DEATH OF A SHERIFF

'The hell!' Stanton lifted to his feet with the little Remington over-and-under in his hand. The muzzle spat flame and Vance Cobly went back with a .41 calibre ball plucking his life out of his belly. The slug hit him directly over the scar on his stomach. It puckered the lips of the old wound inwards . . . then he jerked back as the slug smashed against a rib and deflected upwards . . . Cobly's hand dropped away from the butt of his Remington as he went down on his knees . . .

He shook his head.

Said, 'Lizzy', and then his eyes closed.

D1512782

BREED:
Spanish Gold

JAMES A. MUIR

SPHERE BOOKS LIMITED
30–32 Grays Inn Road, London WC1X 8JL

First published by Sphere Books Ltd 1981
Copyright © James A. Muir 1981

Set in Intertype Baskerville

Printed in Canada

Like Azul, he's a killer on the draw.
This one is for Colin Backhouse,
with thanks.

CHAPTER ONE

Billy Eagle was drunk the day he discovered the mine.

A week earlier he was trading deer meat with a Mexican storekeeper who ran a post on the north reach of the San Pedro, where it ran into the Gila, and picking up just enough money to stock his pack horse with necessaries. Most of Billy's necessaries came bottled fresh from the Mexican's still, the remainder was barely sufficient to see the halfbreed through the next month of hunting. But Billy Eagle didn't worry too much about that : he had cartridges for the old Henry repeater, so he could live off the land if need be. What he did worry about was getting clear of the post before he drank too much and gave the Mexican, or one of his tame Indians, a chance to steal him blind.

He loaded the pack horse and climbed astride the buckskin mustang, heading southwards down the San Pedro before cutting off east in the direction of the Piñon Llanos range. It was a good place to hunt, up there. Far enough away from the settlements springing up all over the Arizona Territory, and clear of the traditional hunting grounds of the Bedonkohe Apache. Billy was part Mimbreño, the son of a Nedni woman and a Mexican father, dark enough to pass as a member of either race, but too heavy in the chest and too bowed of leg to be a true Mexican; yet too aquiline of feature to be a true Apache. Thus he belonged to neither racial group, and was looked down on by the white Americans.

He had chosen to live alone, hunting deer in the ranges south of the Gila. Selling the meat and the hides for sufficient money to buy himself supplies, rot-gut whisky, and the occasional whore. On the whole, he enjoyed the life : he didn't like people too much, and when it got too lonely he could always find a *rancheria,* or go down to the trading post, or into Chandler's Butte.

He followed the course of a little stream called the Mamacita into the foothills, then circled around a bit to confuse his trail. There was no particular reason for that, except innate caution and the knowledge that there were still some Bedonkohe in the hills ready to kill for the whisky he carried.

When he was confident he was neither followed nor watched, he cut due east and began to climb the ragged slopes towards his regular camp. It was located above a cut in the rocks that shaded a small mountain meadow. There was a spring at one end of the vee-shaped cleft, and lush grass covering the centuries' old spread of soil on the bottom. Billy was too canny to make his camp in so tempting a spot, but the place was too good to forget; so he had found a wide ledge forty feet above the cleft and used that as a permanent base. From there he could watch his animals grazing, confident that the only path to his lair was from below, up a narrow trail too steep for a horse to climb, and commanded by the ledge so that he could pick off any intruders from a safe defensive position.

He unsaddled his animals and fastened a line across the entrance of the cleft. Then he hauled his packs up to the cave on the ledge and started a small, smokeless fire. He set some deer meat to roasting and opened the first bottle.

By the time the sun was faded into the west the

deer meat was ready and the bottle was empty. Billy ate. Belched. And went to sleep.

He woke at dawn. Went down to the spring and bathed. Then he checked the animals, went back to the ledge and checked the Henry. He fried some bacon and sourdough biscuits. Drank some coffee. And looked at the bottles stacked neatly inside the cave.

It was too early yet: he needed to hunt down some fresh meat.

But the bottles looked awfully good. Tempting.

He finished his food thinking about them. And then he scrubbed his plate clean, thinking about them.

And then he drank his coffee, thinking about them.

And then he stood up and went into the cave and opened one.

He coughed out most of the first swallow, and took a second. That went down easier. So he took a third. That tasted a whole lot better: he took a fourth.

By the time the bottle was halfway empty the sun was high up and shining into the cleft. And Billy was ready to go hunting. Anything. He felt good. He corked the bottle and set it, with exaggerated caution, back amongst the others. Then he picked up the Henry and moved north along the ledge. There was an old path down there, near vertical in parts and largely washed out by storms and landslips. Billy Eagle had dug steps over sections and fixed disguised ropes over others so that he could move in and out of the cave fast. In case.

Now he slung the Henry over his shoulder by its rawhide carrying strap and began to haul himself up towards the protective rimrock. Partway up, where a slide had layered loose shale over the slope, there was a game trail. Nothing used it much anymore, the edges ending in a twenty foot drop onto the shale, with the two ends separated by a fifteen foot gap.

On this particular day Billy was surprised to see a big pronghorn buck standing at the northern side of the gap. The deer was watching him, looking down over the edge with inquisitive brown eyes. It was a big animal – the kind Billy wanted to find – with enough meat on it to last him around a month.

He grasped the rope tight in both hands, staring back at the pronghorn as he braced his feet against the shale. The loose chippings had been down long enough for soil to begin to cover the edges of the slide and grass was sprouting there. Billy edged his feet tighter on the grass and began to wonder if he could get a shot off.

Had he been sober he would have known it was impossible. But the Mexican's whiskey and the blazing Arizona sun were taking their toll. If he climbed any higher, the pronghorn would be off and running scared, and he would need to climb all the way to the top. Then cast around for spoor and maybe spend the entire day tracking an animal that might – almost certainly would – be smaller than the big buck.

And back in the cave there were more bottles waiting.

Billy Eagle knuckled his left hand around the rope and used his right to ease the Henry clear of his shoulders. He went down on his knees, driving the caps and his toes into the loose soil overlaying the shale. He hooked his left elbow over the rope and opened his left hand just long enough to grab the barrel of the repeater. Then he worked the lever to pump a cartridge into the chamber.

The pronghorn went on staring at him, mildly

curious at the strange antics of the man thirty feet below.

Billy lifted the rifle slowly to his shoulder and sighted along the barrel, lining the flat vee of the hindsight with the upright of the muzzle blade. It would have to be a low shot, angled upwards into the buck's chest. If it came off, he might have to climb up and get across to the game trail before he could send the buck down. Which wouldn't be too difficult : a kick, and the animal would slide most of the way to the ledge.

He fired.

The pronghorn's head went back, forelimbs lifting from the edge of the trail as the .36 calibre slug ploughed into the chest just right of the breastbone. Rictus and instinctive action combined to bunch the powerful hindquarters and propel the deer outwards across the gap.

The animal didn't make it.

Billy's shot had taken out the heart, and even as the effort was made, death was numbing the responses of the limbs. The buck landed two feet clear of the facing edge and crashed down onto the shale. Close on two hundred pounds of deadweight hit the dirt with a thud that reverberated under Billy's feet.

And then the avalanche began.

The buck was still kicking as it slid down towards the halfbreed. The hooves dug against the loose soil and as the spine arched, the horns prodded in, twisting the deer over so that it began to somersault down the slope. At the same time, the earth and shale got disturbed enough that a slide started. Billy Eagle felt the ground move under him and began to swing down the rope in a desperate attempt to reach the safety of the overhung ledge before he was swept away.

He was too slow.

There was a sudden swell from under him and he was torn clear of the rope, rolling down the slope with his eyes and mouth and nose filled with dust, his ears with a low growling sound. The Henry was smashed from his hands and he curled into a protective ball, dragging his knees up against his chest as he fastened both his arms over his head.

Maybe it was because he was partially drunk, or perhaps it was just pure good luck, but he wasn't killed.

There was darkness and pain, and a dream-like feeling of falling with sound all around. Like rolling through the centre of a thunderstorm. Then a blow that smashed the air from his lungs and left him gasping from want of breath as he felt weight against his back and the hot drip of blood in his mouth.

And then it was ended.

Billy Eagle opened his eyes and took his arms from around his head. He rolled over, right hand stretching out to explore his surroundings. He thought he might be dead, but his clouded vision told him that he was on the ledge below the shale slope. His tongue told him he was cut, but when he checked his teeth he found them all in place. And when he checked his body, his hands told him he was very, very lucky.

He got up on his knees.

The slope had assumed a different shape. Instead of the wide fan of grass-covered shale, there was now a deep gap, cut down maybe twenty feet into the rock. The entire deposit of shale had slid clear, taking with it both the pronghorn and the halfbreed's rifle. Most of the rubble had lifted fully clear of the slope, washing a secondary fan over the lower rim, leaving just enough spread across the ledge to halt Billy's descent and death. The ropes he had set so carefully were torn away, just a few ragged ends drooping like vines over the sheer walls of the new split.

Billy stood up, dusting off his shirt and face as he cursed the whiskey he had drunk and wondered how he could find enough money to buy a new gun. His pants were torn and his shirt was tattered. His hands stung where sharp fragments of stone had opened the flesh. And his nose gave out a steady dripping of blood. He blew hard through his nostrils, then pinched them tight and lifted his head back.

And saw the cave.

It was ten feet down from where the pronghorn had stood watching him. There was a series of rough steps going down to the entrance. Very steep and very narrow. The entrance was no more than eight feet across, as many high. And where the slanting sunlight angled against the wall, there was the glint of metal.

It took Billy Eagle close on three hours to get sufficient rope to clamber down the vertical face to where the steps began, but it was time well spent.

He went into the cave with an unlit torch in his hand. And then sat down, staring round at his find.

The cave ran back for fifteen feet before the tunnel opened into a chamber around thirty feet long by as many wide and high. There were two skeletons inside the main chamber, the bones yellow with age and crumbly to the touch. They had kettle-pot helmets settled low over the dried-out craniums, and rusting breast-plates on the ribs. There was a dagger between the bones of one skeleton, put in from the side, between the forwards and rearwards sections of the armour, where they would have been joined together by straps had the leather not rotted away. The other

7

collection of bones had a wide, round hole directly above and between the eyes. The back of the skull was fragmented so that the rusting helmet sat askew the dead head. There was a dent in the rock behind, and faint rust marks running down.

Billy Eagle ignored the skeletons. His torch, lit now against the dark, shone on gleaming metal. It had once been packed in cases of leather and wood, but the original materials were long-gone into corpescent rot, spilling apart to reveal the contents.

Gold, mostly. Smelted down to ingots. The size of his hand; the thickness of his fingers. He didn't know much about gold, but he knew he had hit lucky when he tried to kill the pronghorn buck.

Knew he was rich.

There were jewels, too. Fist-sized opals, and chunks of polished quartz that would buy him a week with any of the whores up at the trading post. More stones that just shone in the torch light, very bright, with little sparkling dances of illumination radiating from their facets.

He threw those away: who wanted glass? And went back to his camp with four of the flat gold bars inside his shirt.

And got very drunk.

Five days later, Billy Eagle showed up at the assay office in Chandler's Butte.

The town was four days clear of the Piñon Llanos and Billy Eagle had taken care to overlay his trail. He wasn't sure how much the gold was worth, but he didn't want anyone else jumping his claim. Not with that much gold sitting inside the cave, waiting for him.

'Christ Jesus!' The clerk lifted the chippings from the scales. 'That works out to around eighty per cent pure.'

'How much?' asked Billy Eagle.

'That block?' The clerk shrugged. 'One hundred dollars.'

'All right,' said the halfbreed. 'I got three more.'

The clerk choked. He reached up to loosen his string tie with his lips working like fighting caterpillars.

'Show me.'

His voice was hoarse, and got hoarser still as Billy Eagle dropped the ingots onto the desk. He used a scalpel to flake off pieces from each bar and then dropped the flakes into a pan of acid. After the seeth had cooled, he dunked them in a second mixture and then weighed the residue.

His eyes got wider still.

'Oh, my God!' he said. 'Where'd you find this?'

Billy Eagle grinned and pressed a finger to his lips.

'You got near enough one thousand dollars' worth of gold there,' said the clerk. 'Christ! That's akin to the Sutter's Mill rush. Jesus!'

'Who buys it?' asked Billy. 'You?'

'Mister,' said the clerk, 'I'll buy. How much you want?'

'Tell me,' said Billy. 'I don't know.'

The clerk swallowed some more, his adam's apple bouncing up and down his throat like like a blind-bob at a county fair. He seemed to be choking on it as his eyes shifted wide inside the sockets and a sheen of sweat spread over his face.

'Look,' he said, 'I hafta to go raise the money. Here.' He tugged two five dollar bills from his vest. 'Go have a drink on me in the Little Sister. It's right across the street. You just order whatever you want. If that don't cover it, I'll be back to settle the bill.'

'How much?' repeated Billy Eagle. 'For the gold?'

'Oh, God!' The clerk's throat began to look like it was trying to climb up inside his mouth. 'One thousand. Straight cash.'

'You got a deal,' said Billy Eagle. 'I'll wait for you.'

The clerk came out from behind the desk and opened the door. He waited long enough for the half-breed to cross the street and enter the saloon. Then he locked the assay office and went out by the back way, stumbling through the back alleys of Chandler's Butte to the hotel. The only hotel. It was called The Hotel, with a sign out in front to prove it.

The owner was in his private room. The one customers never reached. It was cool and quiet, the shutters closed just enough that the sun didn't come in but the breeze could. To stir the fan centred on the ceiling.

There were two men outside the door. One fat, one thin. Both ugly. Both mean-looking. Both armed like gunmen; or bodyguards.

'I gotta see Mister Stanton,' said the clerk. 'It's real important.'

'He's sleepin',' said Jimmy Witt. 'Don't wanna be disturbed.'

The clerk looked at the gigantic man. Took in the red hair and the pale face. The cut-down shotgun on the strap over his right shoulder. And swallowed breath.

'He'll want to know about this,' he said. 'Honest.'

'What is it?' asked the second man, almost soft. 'Tell us.'

He was dressed in a frilled shirt that must have cost

him a lot of money back in St. Louis. Probably as much as the sateen vest and the tight-fitted black pants that sat snug over the grainy, hand-tooled boots.

He wore a pair of matched Smith & Wesson Schofields either side of his lean hips, his slender frame contrasting with the massive bulk of the other guard. His hands, though, stayed close to the guns, belying the gentleness of his voice.

'Money,' said the clerk. 'Jesus! I never seen so much.'

'Let him in,' said Art Durant. 'This sounds interesting.'

The red haired giant nodded and tapped on the door. With his knuckles, it was like hearing a club banged on a hollow drum.

The door opened and a harsh, dry voice said, 'What is it?'

'Man to see you,' rasped Witt.

'About money,' added Durant. 'Says it's a lot.'

The door opened and the clerk got shoved through by one of Witt's enormous paws. He stumbled inside, fighting to keep his balance as he stared at the cadaver face of Cole Stanton.

The man was tall and thin as a marble tombstone. His face was sucked in around the eyes and mouth so that he resembled a skull. His skin was marble pale, dry as bleached bones, with eyes that were sunk deep into sockets rimmed with black that matched the colour of the pupils. He wore a black suit : black coat that matched the pants and the vest. Black, buttoned boots. A black string tie. The only colour on him came from his shirt and face. They were both white; almost the same colour.

'Well?'

It was all he said.

The clerk's adam's apple began to bob up and down again.

'A man come in just now.' He paused. 'Sir! an' handed me close on three thousand dollars' worth of Spanish gold. A halfbreed, he was.'

'So?' Cole Stanton lifted a silk handkerchief to his mouth and coughed up some phlegm. 'What's that to do with me?'

He examined the kerchief as he waited for the clerk's reply.

'You want to invest around here, don't you? Sir?' The clerk watched the thin man's face for hope of an affirmative reply. 'This could be good. I got the man waiting in the Little Sister. I said I'd buy his gold for one thousand dollars. Maybe fifteen hundred.'

'So buy it,' said Stanton. 'It sounds like a good investment.'

'I don't have anything near that,' wailed the clerk. 'I need you to bank me.'

'Why?' asked Stanton. 'I came out here for my health. I already own this hotel and two saloons. Why chance money on a nowhere strike?'

'Christ Jesus!' said the clerk. 'That gold was damn' near pure. It has to come from one of the old Spanish caches. It was ingots! Not placer gold; not a vein. That means there's a whole stack back in the hills that only that halfbreed knows about.'

'So?' said Stanton. 'What do you want me to do?'

'Bank me,' said the clerk. 'I can buy that gold for one thousand dollars. Fifteen hundred at the most. It's worth at least twice that. More, if he brings fresh bars in.'

Stanton thought for a moment, wiping his silk kerchief delicately over his lips.

'All right,' he said at last. 'I'll bank you one thousand. We split the profits after that.'

And the Billy Eagle strike got to be a legend.

Like the Dutchman, or the Eldorado.

And either way, the Mimbreño halfbreed began to get rich on the gold he brought in to Chandler's Butte.

Once a month he came in, delivering a few more gold bars to the assay office to sell them for half their real worth. Cole Stanton and the clerk began to get rich enough that both of them wondered where the halfbreed was finding the ingots. Stanton was already rich; the clerk was poor. Until now. And the idea of getting as rich as Stanton made him greedy.

So one night he suffered an accident.

He hadn't said much about his new-found wealth. Just taken Billy Eagle's gold and changed it for Stanton's money, then worked a deal to get the ingots melted down into random chunks before Stanton had them shipped east on the stage line he owned, so they could be sold through the thin man's various companies beyond the Missouri and the money funneled back to Chandler's Butte. Mostly in clean, new notes.

But one night, when the clerk's profits topped the five thousand dollar mark, he had gone over the top along with his makings. He had gone out and got drunk, shooting off his mouth about his new-found fortune.

The next morning he was found in an alley with his skull crushed under what might have been the wheels of a metal-shod buggy. Or the backstrap of a shotgun.

Either way, the death was put down to an accident.

And no one asked Cole Stanton about the killing.

There wasn't that much point: Stanton was a respectable businessman, just the kind of man the

Arizona Territory needed to make it as respectable as him. He had already invested a lot of money. He owned The Hotel, and the Little Sister saloon; half the mortgages on the small properties around the town and outside; he had put up at least half of Sheriff Cobly's campaign fund, and now he was promising to bring a school – complete with teacher – into town.

No one wanted to cross him or argue with him.

Money was talking all the way down his line.

CHAPTER TWO

Billy Eagle went on bringing his gold in to Chandler's Butte because it was the closest town with an assay office and a bank that would transform the gold into ready cash. It was also the closest town prepared to serve a halfbreed with whiskey and whores.

He didn't think much about it; just enjoyed his new-found riches and rode out after each five-day drunk into the hills. He still took care to cover his tracks, because by now people were asking him questions all the time. About where his gold came from, and how had he found it, and where was it?

But Billy Eagle was too smart to fall for that. Even when he was staggering on rubber legs with his eyes like egg-filled glasses that rolled loose about the sockets.

Far too smart.

He'd just get up on his buckskin pony and amble out of town. Maybe only a few miles out before he fell off and spent the night with the pony pissing on his legs and his snores disturbing the prairie chickens and the coyotes. But he still woke in time to get mounted and hit the hills before the men following him caught his tracks. And like the old days – before he got rich – he still circled round and lost anyone tailing him.

So he kept his secret mine hidden.

Which angered Cole Stanton a great deal.

Stanton had come West to preserve his health. He was consumptive, threatened with rotting lungs should he not move to a drier climate than St. Louis. He had studied a map of the western states and picked out Chandler's Butte for no other reason than that it was high on the east flank of the Piñon Llanos range, with branches of a near-defunct stage line going into the town, which was close enough to the Gila to keep him in touch with his interests in California. He had bought out the stage line, renaming it the Stanton, Arizona & Western Line, then bought out half the town.

Now he owned the S.A.W. line, the Little Sister saloon, The Hotel, a sizeable portion of the bank, and the livery stable. By threatened default on half the mortgages in Chandler's Butte, he also could lay claim to at least nine stores and seventeen houses.

He was rich.

And like most rich men, he was greedy: in his thinking, money bred money, and the ones who didn't have it didn't deserve it.

He wanted Billy Eagle's strike.

He couldn't see why a drunken halfbreed had any kind of right to that kind of wealth. Christ Jesus! the man could hardly speak English, and he certainly didn't know the value of gold. If he did, he'd have sold it far higher than Stanton was paying through the new clerk at the assay office. God! He'd three times offered the filthy halfbreed more money than the bastard could hope to earn in his lifetime.

And the man had refused him on every offer!

A stinking, goddam halfbreed!

A bitch Apache whelp out of a sungrinner Mex!

Barely human. More like an animal. Some slinking creature that dug its nose in offal and came up with real men's pickings.

Like gold.

And Christ Jesus! What an awful lot of gold!

Cole Stanton lifted his silk handkerchief to his mouth and coughed delicately as Billy Eagle came out of Dan Sutter's store. He watched the halfbreed load his ugly grey pack horse with whiskey and supplies, and then climb astride the buckskin mustang. He watched Billy drop the new-bought Winchester .44-40 into the California loop holster and drum his heels against the mustang's sides.

Jesus! The man didn't even wear decent boots. Just Apache-style moccasins that reached up to his knees with the laces hanging down like tattered cloth.

Stanton lowered his kerchief and raised a pale left hand.

Jimmy Witt appeared beside him like a genie springing from a bottle.

'I want him followed,' said the man with the tombstone face. 'Send Donny and Osmond. I want to know where he's going.'

Jimmy Witt ducked his massive head in unspoken reply, and went back inside the saloon.

Thirty minutes later the two Mormons were heeling their horses out of Chandler's Butte in pursuit of Billy Eagle.

They covered the first part of the trail fast, knowing that the halfbreed would flank the Condame creek down to the south before swinging into the hills. After that, they weren't sure, but Osmond was pretty good at tracking and, anyway, they figured their man to swing up into the Piñon Llanos range and climb for the high country. They swung west and south, angling to cut across Billy Eagle's trail to fade him and pick up his tracks when they were more certain.

Night fell, and they made cold camp.

In the morning they located fresh spoor and the tracks of two horses. One unshod; like a mustang a halfbreed Apache might ride. They followed on.

The trail lifted up towards the western rimrock of the Piñon range, drifting through heavy stands of timber that shaded the way like shutters brought down to cut out the sun.

The two men began to climb the trail with Donny in the lead, moving slowly as he scanned the ground for sign. He was a young man, barely into his twenties, with a set of tombstone teeth that he flashed constantly in a weak-mouthed grin and a lot of glossy black hair. He fancied himself as a gunfighter, and dressed in accordance with the popular conception of that breed : black shirt, black pants, black boots. A silver-tooled black belt spanning his narrow waist with two pearl-handled Colt's .45 Peacemakers strapped to his thighs. A short-brimmed black hat with a snakeskin band shaded his dark eyes.

Osmond was older, less fancy and far more dangerous. He was around thirty-five, with lazy, near-yellow eyes and a knife scar puckering his left cheek from ear to mouth. He slumped in his saddle, riding with the lazy indifference of a man long accustomed to spending hours on horseback. His brown cotton shirt was dark with sweat under the arms and down the back, and he kept removing the battered Texas stetson he wore to wipe a greasy bandanna over his totally bald skull. There was a plain Colt's Peacemaker in a scratched holster hung cross-draw style on his left hip, and the scabbard slung alongside his saddle held the stock of a Sharps buffalo rifle. He was chewing the stub of a dead cigar.

Donny halted, slipping from the saddle to peer

closer at the trail. Osmond waited with the bored patience of a man who's seen it all and expects to see most of it again.

'Bastard's swung off into the trees.' Donny stood up, staring at the surrounding cottonwoods. 'He could know we're followin' him.'

'Shit!' Osmond spat the soggy remnants of the cigar onto the ground between them. 'I figgered that all on my lonesome.'

Donny bristled. 'You're so goddam smart, you say where he's headed.'

'I knew that, kid, I'd be there waitin' for him.' Osmond lifted his canteen to his mouth. 'I'd cache me some o' that Spanish gold an' take the rest back to Cole. Then I'd quit an' head back to Utah. Pick me a few wives an' live high on the hog.'

'Screw Utah!' grinned the younger man. 'Me, I'd head for New Orleans. Maybe St. Louis. Shit! I got some o' that gold, I'd buy me a river boat an' sail up an' down between the two with a crew o' fancy women.'

'Wishin' ain't worth whistlin' at a pig,' grunted Osmond, mopping his bald head again. 'Trouble is, we don't know where the gold is at. So we gotta find the 'breed.'

'He went that way.' Donny pointed off to the left. 'Moved into the trees.'

Osmond nodded, staring at the shadowy flanks of the ridge. Inside the timber it would be easy for the halfbreed to circle back and come round behind them, or from the flank. Old Billy was a drunken son-ofabitch, but he knew his woodcraft; like most of the heathen redmen. And he could take care of himself. Osmond didn't relish the idea of trailing into an ambush: he liked it the other way around. He stared up the slope to where the trail gave out onto a plateau.

'Well?' asked Donny. 'We goin' after him, or not?'

'We're goin' after him,' nodded Osmond, 'but we're goin' careful. That ole 'breed ain't stupid. But nor am I.'

'*We*,' corrected Donny.

Osmond ignored the correction, pointing up the rise: 'We go that way. Try to spot him from the top.'

They set off up the slope. It was steep, angling through the cottonwoods with stands of oak and maple interspersed through the canyons, shading the trail so that it was not until they reached the summit that the sun shone fully through the overhang of leaves. They crested the rise and halted again. A half mile spread of grass angled out in front of them, banded to the south by the trees, ending to the north where a secondary fold of hills lifted up towards the peaks. To the west, a grassy knoll rose high as a two-storey house from the otherwise flat meadow. They galloped towards it.

Atop the knoll, Osmond dragged field glasses from his saddlebags and began to scan the lower slopes. It was impossible to obtain a clear view of the land below, but every so often the trees broke up – where a meadow opened the ground, or landslips had cleared a section – so he was able to spot parts of the interlacing game trails below him. He swung the glasses slowly from left to right, then back again; repeating the motion over and over until he found what he was looking for.

'I got him,' he said; softly. 'About three hundred yards down, moving across a slide. Goin' slow.'

He passed the field glasses to Donny. The younger Mormon trailed in on Osmond's pointing finger, adjusting the sights to his own vision.

Billy Eagle was walking his mustang very slowly

over a wide fan of shale, turning to urge the pack horse on. It was difficult going, because the slope was loose, the two horses sinking fetlock deep into the gravel, the hindquarters of the loaded pack horse skirling streamers of stone down the angle of the slope. It was several hundred yards wide, and the halfbreed wasn't halfway across yet.

'What we do?' asked Donny. 'Head him off?'

'Too late.' Osmond shook his head. 'Time we got down there, he'd be long gone.' He pointed across to the timber flanking the shale. 'He'd lose us again in that.'

'So?' Donny handed back the field glasses. 'What's our next move?'

Osmond took the glasses and went over the far side of the knoll to where their horses were cropping grass. He thrust the glasses back inside his saddlebag and pulled out a long cylinder of blued metal with glass shining at either end. Then he slid the Sharps from the scabbard and clambered back up the slope. He flattened out, peering through the optical sight as he made careful adjustments, then snapped it in place atop the rifle. He sat down on the grass, crossing his ankles and lifting his knees. He rested both elbows on his knees and brought the stock of the Sharps up to his shoulder, settling one yellow eye tight against the rear of the sight. His left closed. He reached up, making a further correction.

His thumb pulled the hammer back, and he took a deep, slow breath.

'You ever hear about Billy Dixon?' he asked. 'At Adobe Walls?'

'No.' Donny shook his head. 'Why?'

'I beat him twice on target shoots,' murmured Osmond.

'So?' Donny shrugged. 'What's that mean?'

'Forget it,' said the older man.

And took a second slow breath.

The muzzle of the Sharps moved fractionally as the breath eased gently clear of Osmond's narrow lips, and his right forefinger took up the trigger slack.

He went on squeezing until all the slack was taken up, then took another breath and let it slowly out through his parted lips as his finger tightened down against the resistance of the hammer spring. The trigger closed. The hammer thudded forward, the stud striking the percussion cap so that ignited fulminate flashed fire down the channel and the linen cartridge detonated. 120 grains of black powder exploded the lead slug from the muzzle as a terrific thunderclap echoed over the hills.

Billy Eagle heard the sound, and turned his face up the slope.

Then he felt his mustang go out from under him as blood sprayed from the right shoulder, and a second, thicker, gout burst from the leftside ribs.

The .54 calibre ball mashed the pony's shoulder-blade into fragments, continuing on through the chest to burst the lungs and shatter the left foreleg. The pony screamed and went down on its face, pitching the halfbreed over the falling head so that he landed six feet clear of the flailing body. The pony went on screaming as it rolled on its back and began to slide down the slope, dragging the pack horse behind it.

Billy Eagle got up on his knees with his Colt in his hand. Then he cursed and thrust the handgun back inside the holster : he knew now what the thunderclap meant.

He slithered down through the shale and managed to snatch his Winchester clear of the saddle before the mustang writhed on down the shale. He dragged a knife from his belt and slashed through the lead rein connecting the dead animal to the pack horse.

The mustang was kicking up a cloud of dust as the halfbreed manhandled the pack horse across the slope, fighting his way through the clinging grit in a desperate attempt to avoid both the next shot and the threatening landslip. The shale beneath him was starting to shift as the mustang went down in a dust-curling slide, churning the loose gravel into runnels that poured away down the slope, opening fans of emptiness that got filled with rock from higher up. Billy Eagle forgot about the hidden marksman as the more immediate problem of the impending avalanche threatened to sweep him away.

Osmond laughed out loud and headed back to his horse.

'Come on!' he yelled to Donny. 'We got time to get in front of him now.'

The black-clad youngster ran for his horse, his even teeth spread in a huge grin.

They got mounted and rode hard to the north, angling for a break in the trees that would take them down the rise to catch Billy Eagle as he emerged from the shale.

The thunderclap of the Sharps was instantly recognised by the lone rider higher up the slope. He had heard that kind of sound too many times before to mistake it for anything other than a gun shot, and while there was no reason he should take any interest in whatever was happening below him he still felt instinctive curiosity. He swung astride his horse and began to move down towards the echo.

He was a tall man, wide-shouldered and leanly hipped. His body was lithe, deceptively muscled under a mane of sun-bleached hair that fell in white-gold straightness from the confines of a wide, flat-crowned Sonoran stetson. He wore a shirt that had once been white linen, and was now near-colourless, with a dark leather vest on top. Buckskin pants that fitted snug against his thighs and were tucked into knee-high Chiricahua moccasins. The hilt of a slender-bladed throwing knife protruded from the top of the right moccasin. There was a Colt's .45 calibre Frontier model hung cross-draw on his left hip, and a heavy leather sheath on his right. The sheath held a wide-bladed Bowie knife. His face was a mixture of white and Apache bloodlines: the wide mouth and heavy lips attesting his mother's parentage, the firm, straight nose and cold blue eyes, his father's.

His mother had been a woman of the Chiricahua. Rainbow Hair, kin to the great Mangas Colorado. His father had been a Santa Fé trader, Kieron Gunn. Both were dead now, killed by scalphunters.

The man was known by several names.

In the Chiricahua *rancheria* where he grew to manhood, he was called Azul, for his cold blue eyes. In the cathedral in Santa Fé, he had been christened Matthew Gunn, after his father.

Around the border country they called him Breed. And the men who knew him took care not to cross him, remembering the legend that grew around him. Remembering a word that was synonymous with Breed: Death.

He carried it with him, they said. Part Chiricahua Apache, part white, he killed whoever stood against him. And the hatred he engendered killed those he befriended. He was a man alone: belonging to neither the world of the redmen, nor that of the white. Travelling his own path. Breed spells death, they said around the border country, walk away from him. Or die.

He slid the Winchester rifle sheathed in his saddle boot out and levered a shell into the breech in a single, fluid movement. Then he rode on, the Winchester balanced against his right hip as he guided the big grey horse with his left hand and his knees. The horse went down the slope at an easy canter, finding its ground easily. It was a handsome animal; like its owner, a mixture of ancestors. There was Arab in the set of the head and the clean lines of the body; Morgan in the depth of chest and strength of limbs; mustang in the casual litheness with which it negotiated the slope, cat-sure and fleetly silent.

After the single shot there was a long silence, and the man called Breed began to wonder if he was reacting too strongly to some innocent hunting party. He decided not. These hills lay within the domain of Apacheria, and few Indians possessed the heavy calibre Sharps rifles. Equally, the game to be found here – pronghorns, mule deer, and the like – were too small to warrant that kind of firepower. The Sharps was a long-distance weapon, capable of bringing down a full-grown buffalo with a single shot : smaller animals would be torn up by the slug. A deer hit by a .54 calibre bullet would be useless to an Apache, the meat pulped and the hide ripped. And the Apaches were nothing if not brutally practical. No, it would be a whiteman – a *pinda-lick-oyi* – using that gun.

And the sixth sense developed over the years of living close to death was nibbling at his mind like a rat trapped in a corn crib.

The premonition was born out by the sharper blast

of a Winchester and the staccato rattle of handguns fired in unison.

He moved farther down the slope, halting the grey stallion inside a break of junipers that hid the big horse in dappled shadow and low-hanging branches. He slid from the saddle and left the horse ground hitched, continuing on foot. Slipping silently and near-invisible through the trees. Like a cougar on the stalk.

As he descended towards the source of the gun fire, the sounds resolved into a distinct pattern that granted his danger-tuned ears a clear image of the events below him. There were two men to his right, one a hundred yards higher up the slope than his companion. They were using the Sharps and the two handguns respectively. Over to his left, and slightly below the other two, a third man was returning their fire with a Winchester .44-40.

When he reached the edge of a spill and crouched in the shadow of a big cottonwood, the impression was confirmed. There was a shale-filled bowl, surrounded on three sides by trees, cut off at the lowest point by a near-vertical drop. A dead mustang was attracting flies on the edge of the drop, and three-quarters of the way over the bowl, a man was bellied down behind a shallow outcrop of reddish stone. There was a pack horse on its side behind him, lead rein looped over the forelimbs to hold it still. The man was short and heavy-chested, with thick, black hair dragged off his face by a scarlet bandanna. His features showed the same mixture of racial origins that set Breed apart from Apache and white alike : he was dark, with the high, wide cheekbones of an Apache, and the same deep-set, dark eyes, but his nose and mouth betrayed traces of Mexican blood.

He was dressed in a dirty yellow shirt worn outside dark blue pants that were tucked into flat-soled Apache moccasins. A round-crowned hat with a flat brim and a circlet of silver conchos was hung on his back, and he had a gunbelt with a Colt's .45 buckled over his shirt. He was firing the Winchester.

As Breed watched, chips of stone erupted from the outcrop as the Sharps boomed again. When the half-breed lifted up to trigger the rifle, two handguns rattled shots in his direction, driving him back behind his cover.

There was a pause, and a voice yelled: 'We got you dead, Billy! Throw out yore guns an' move out slow.'

The reply was gutteral, thick with the accents of Apacheria and too much whiskey, but clear enough: 'Go to hell!'

The Sharps boomed again, the slug ricochetting off the stone with a whine like an angry hornet. The Winchester plucked a fall of bright green leaves from a spruce. And the two Colts fountained dirt a yard to the halfbreed's left.

'Tell us where it is,' shouted a second voice. 'We'll let you go.'

'I ain't drunk,' roared the man called Billy. 'I don't believe pigs can fly.'

The retort brought a volley of fire that sent him ducking against the shale behind the rock. Breed began to move sideways in the direction of the man with the Sharps.

He cat-footed through the timber, pausing where the lightning-struck bole of a giant oak hung a network of roots over the slope. Twenty feet below him there was a hairless man dressed in faded work clothes thumbing a fresh load into the Sharps. He

27

had an unlit cigar clenched between his teeth, and a Colt holstered on his waist. Breed waited until he had fired the buffalo gun, and then went down the angle of the hill on silent moccasins.

The man was chomping the cigar and sweating profusely as he levered the spent load clear of the breech. Beside him, spread neatly on a flattish section of root, were five fresh loads, and as many percussion caps.

He was closing the breech and reaching for a cap when the muzzle of Breed's Winchester touched the back of his neck. His teeth clamped tight on the unlit cigar, biting through the stem so that a section fell onto the ground under his face. He spat the remaining piece out. He didn't move.

'Keep your hands just where they are.' Breed's voice was low and cold; like frost settling on a coffin. 'Don't shout.'

The man froze.

'Who are you?' Breed asked. 'Who's the other one?'

'Osmond,' said the man. 'My partner's called Donny.'

'And the target?' Breed kept the Winchester pressed against Osmond's neck. 'The one called Billy?'

'Billy Eagle. Ain't nuthin' but a stinkin' halfbreed.'

'Turn around.' Breed's voice stayed low. 'Look at me.'

Osmond turned. And his eyes got wide as he saw Breed's face, the greenish pupils dilating into the yellow of the surrounding orbs. Breed smiled, and it was like looking into an open grave.

'You got something against halfbreeds?' he asked, adjusting the Winchester so that the muzzle dug into Osmond's flat stomach.

'No! Jesus Christ! No, I don't.' Osmond winced as the foresight twisted against his flesh. 'I'm just doin' a job.'

'He wanted?' Breed asked.

'He's got a strike.' The words came fast now as Osmond saw death looking at him. Smiling at him. 'There's a cache of Spanish gold up here someplace. Only Billy Eagle knows where.'

'And halfbreeds don't have the right to own gold,' said Breed; very low. Very cold. 'That right?'

'Look.' Osmond spat shreds of cigar butt. 'We could cut you in. That bastard's rich. Hell! we could even leave him some. There's enough.'

'To share with halfbreeds?' asked the blond-haired man.

And squeezed the trigger.

The Winchester's report was muffled against Osmond's stomach. The bullet smashed through the muscle with terrifying force. Osmond folded like a jacknife under the impact, groaning as nervous shock numbed his senses. The bullet tore through his belly, ripping a massive hole in his intestines so that as it came out through his back he humped upwards from the ground. It burst his stomach apart, loosening his bladder and bowels so that urine stained the front of his faded pants and a sudden spurt of faeces overrode the cordite smell. Blood spread in a wide swathe from under his back and he rolled on his side, face touching his knees as he curled into a foetal ball. As he turned, Breed saw the gigantic hole in his shirt. It was the size of a man's spread hand, rimmed with lips of ruptured flesh, all red, with straggly pieces of the internal organs bursting from the gap.

Osmond pressed his elbows against his sides, trying to lift his hands to the smaller hole in the front of his body. He coughed, spitting out strands of cigar butt and long streamers of blood. Breed snatched the Colt from the holster and tossed it away into the trees. Sweat glistened on Osmond's bald skull, and blood-stained spittle flecked his lips.

Breed swiped his hand over the root carrying the cartridges, then tore the cap away from the nipple of the Sharps. He lifted the heavy rifle and drove the muzzle deep into the earth, grinding it round so that the bore got filled with dirt. Then he tossed it aside and moved back into the trees.

'Osmond?' Donny's voice rang out from lower down the slope. 'You all right?'

Silence : like night falling on a cold timber camp in winter. Then a scream.

It was high and shrill, hitting the upper registers of a man's vocal cords before it bubbled down into a gut-wrenching moaning sound.

'Osmond!' Donny yelled. 'Fer God's sake! You all right?'

The scream echoed again. Lower this time, as if the cords of the throat were riven and washed in blood. It broke off into a coughing fit.

'Oh, Jesus!'

The man who said it stood up, turning to scan the slope with two pearl-handled Colts cocked and ready. He was dressed in black, his hat on the ground beside him so that Breed could see all of his glossy black hair. His mouth was open as he shouted, exposing clean, white teeth between the fleshy lips.

Breed lifted the Winchester to his shoulder and closed his finger on the trigger.

The teeth exploded into fragments of sparkling enamel and blood-washed ivory. Donny's head jerked back, a terrific fountain of crimson erupting from his neck. Both handguns went off, blasting useless shots against the sky as the .44-40 calibre slug tore out the rear of his mouth and ploughed on through his windpipe. It ruptured the vital linkage of air to the brain, so that Donny's big, dark eyes snapped shut, then opened, staring blankly at the empty sky. It nicked the bones connecting his body to his brain, setting up a nervous reaction that danced him backwards like a puppet on a string. His whole body twitched, fingers snapping on the triggers of the pearl-handled Colts as his thumbs flopped free of the hammers. Blood ran down over his jaw, and from his nostrils, staining the mangled, perfect teeth. A heel caught in a root, and he pitched over on his back. The impact gouted a fresh spurt of blood from his mouth, and his bootheels dug into the loam, stretching his body out as both arms jerked vertical at the sky.

The pearl handled Colts drooped from his hands. They caught on his forefingers, still hooked through the trigger guards. Sun's light flashed off the polished metal. Then the arms dropped to either side and the pistols flew clear. Donny stretched his length over the ground. Where his head landed there was a circle of steaming, crimson blood. A fly landed on his throat. Then he twitched again, disturbing the hungry insect. His heels dug against the ground and his head lifted over and back. His spine arched for a moment, lifting the body like a drawn bow. Then an awful trembling shook his body and thick gouts of blood fountained from his mouth and neck. And the body went limp, slumping down with a tired sigh, like an old man rolling onto a feather mattress.

The flies descended in thick clouds.

Breed worked his way back up the slope.

Osmond was on his left side, curled into a tight ball with his fingers interlaced over the hole in his belly. His knees were up tight against his stomach, and there were thick streamers of blood-stained mucus drying over his nose and mouth. A dark balloon of flies covered the hole in his back.

Breed cradled the Winchester in his arms and drifted round to upper side of the shale drop. Still wary.

'Billy Eagle!' he shouted. 'You alive?'

'Yeah!' was the only answer.

'They're dead,' Breed hollered. 'Both of them. I killed them.'

'Who are you?'

'Azul.' He wondered if the halfbreed knew the name. 'That's what my mother called me. My father got me christened Matthew. Matthew Gunn.'

'Breed?' Billy Eagle's voice was doubting. 'The one they call Breed?''

'I guess,' he shouted. 'Like you. Part Apache.'

'Jesus!' said Billy Eagle. '*Jesus Cristo!* Thanks.'

He came over the shale with the Winchester in his right hand, dragging the pack horse behind him. Breed waited until he was clear of the slip, standing back inside the trees with the rifle angled over his left shoulder.

Billy Eagle dragged the horse up into the timber and dropped the Winchester into the loops of the pack saddle.

'You saved my life, I guess,' he said. 'You want a drink?'

Breed shook his head. Billy took a bottle out and tipped a long swallow down his throat.

'Who were they?' he asked.

'One was called Donny,' said Breed. 'The other, Osmond.'

'Donny. Osmond.' Billy Eagle grinned. 'They sure sung sweet.'

CHAPTER THREE

The two men faced one another across the glow of the fire.

Billy Eagle drank whiskey, taking three swallows for each time he passed the bottle over to Breed.

'What do I call you?' he asked. 'Way I heard the story, you got three names.'

'Azul will do,' said the halfbreed. 'Call me Azul.'

'Sure.' Billy emptied the bottle and set it carefully aside. 'I'll do that. It don't mean we're friends, though. I ain't showing you, nor no one else, where the mine's hid.'

Azul shrugged. 'I'm not interested. Keep it.'

Billy Eagle nodded with the sage and whiskey-influenced judgment of a drunkard. 'Right, Azul. That's mine, that mine. Not no one else's. Just mine, the mine. But I wanna pay you for saving me. I always wanna pay my debts.'

'It don't matter,' said Azul. 'Forget it.'

'No.' Billy reached behind him to fumble his saddlebag open. 'Here. You take some money.'

He thrust out a hand filled with bills. Most of them were tens. Azul looked at them, and shook his head.

'It doesn't matter,' he said, slowly; carefully. 'Leave it.'

'Owe you a debt,' mumbled Billy. 'Allus pay my debts. Allus have. Rich now. Pay more. You take it.'

Azul shrugged and lifted fifty dollars from the wad in the drunken halfbreed's hand.

'That's enough,' he said. 'It covers the shells I used.'

Billy Eagle chuckled, his bleary eyes getting slanted up with whiskey-cunning.

'You took m'money. Give a promise that way.' It came out as *Geeaproms atay*. 'Gotta give yore word not to trail me. Kill you if you do.'

It sounded like *killuifadoo*.

Azul shook his head. 'I'm not trailing you. Keep the mine : I ain't interested.'

'Lot are,' grumbled Billy Eagle. 'Too many.'

Azul watched him slump over with his head a foot clear of his saddle. He lifted the man back in place and settled a blanket around the snoring body. Then he drank the last of the coffee and saddled the grey stallion. He didn't feel like staying around a drunk halfbreed. Not riding herd on someone like Billy Eagle. Nor at all interested in the mine : money was too much of a problem.

He walked the big horse clear of the fire and climbed into the saddle. One hour later, he was ten miles clear of Billy Eagle's camp, high up in the Piñon Llanos with a cool breeze blowing over his face and a stream bubbling lazily off to his right. He lay back, looking up at the stars. They were very bright, shining from a sky the colour of midnight velvet. Clear and cool and clean.

He closed his eyes, thinking that with fifty dollars in his pocket he could ride into a town and restock on shells. Buy some food that would see him through a few months of lonely hunting. Billy had said the nearest town was a place called Chandler's Butte, about forty to fifty miles east and south.

He thought he might go there. Maybe even stop over a while.

He went to sleep.

Billy Eagle woke with whiskey bells ringing inside his skull and what felt like a dead mouse curled over his tongue. He blinked at the sky and cursed the brightness, then sat up, holding his aching head. He was surprised to find Azul gone, and decided it was some kind of trick to fool him into pinpointing the cache of gold. He chuckled sagely and began to brew up coffee that he laced with whiskey.

After a while he felt better. Partly because of the whiskey, partly because he had a plan worked out.

Instead of continuing along his original path, he began to backtrack, thinking to throw his imaginary follower off the scent. That was how he returned to the shale slope and saw the bodies. He didn't pay them much attention, but when he saw the glitter of Donny's matched Colts he got interested.

The pistols were Colt's .45 Peacemakers, but very special Peacemakers. In place of the standard gunmetal blue, they were silvered, polished up to a brilliant shine. The foresights had been filed off, leaving smooth barrels, and the triggers were tightened down to a hair-span pull. The butts were pearl, engraved with a pattern of snakes entwined about a capital D on each side. They were the finest looking guns Billy Eagle had ever seen. He picked them up. Tossed his own plain, wood-butted Colt aside, and dropped one of the fancy guns into his holster. The other he tucked into his saddlebags.

That was one of the biggest mistakes Billy Eagle ever made.

A month later his supplies were used up and he decided to go back to Chandler's Butte to re-stock.

He rode the pack horse into town and headed straight for the livery. He got the pack horse stalled up and then bought a tall bay gelding and a big Comstock saddle. He paid forty dollars for the horse and one hundred twenty-five for the saddle; both with ready cash. Then he went to the assay office and traded two more gold bars for seven hundred dollars. With the money in his pockets he booked a room in The Hotel, and headed for the Little Sister saloon.

He enjoyed the way the townsfolk paid him attention now. Enjoyed the way the barkeep had a bottle of the good whiskey uncorking the instant he walked in through the swing doors. More so, the way the saloon girls clustered round him.

He called for drinks on the house, and took his bottle and two girls over to a table.

After a while, Cole Stanton showed up, heading straight for Billy's table.

'Billy.' The tall, cadaverous man doffed his hat. 'Join you?'

'Why not?' Billy started to say *Mister Stanton*, then changed it: 'Sit down, Cole.'

He liked that.

'How you doing?' Stanton called for a fresh bottle. 'Ready to take a partner yet?'

'No.' Billy shook his head. 'Don't need no partner, Mister . . . Cole. What I got, I got on my own. Don't figger to share it.'

Stanton laughed, then raised a silk kerchief to his lips as the laughter turned into a cough. He dabbed tidily at his mouth and swallowed a glass of whiskey.

'Dangerous for a man on his own, Billy. There's a lot of hardcases drifting in on word of what you found.'

'I can handle them,' Billy asserted. 'I done that already.'

'How's that? Stanton poured fresh drinks.

'Shit!' Billy Eagle tossed down his liquor and poured a refill. 'Was two followed me up the last time. They're dead now. Crow bait. Look.'

He hauled the pearl-handled Colt from under his jacket and dumped it on the table. Stanton stared at it.

'I took that an' its twin off of one of 'em,' Billy boasted. 'The other was usin' a big Sharps, but I don't need that kinda gun, so I left it.'

'And you killed them both?' asked Stanton. 'You shot them both dead?'

Billy took another swallow of whiskey and nodded: 'Sure. Both of 'em. Taught 'em what it means to backtrail Billy Eagle.'

Stanton chuckled and made an excuse to leave. He went over to the bar and ordered a fresh bottle for the halfbreed, then walked out through the batwings.

Out on the sidewalk he took a deep breath and mopped his face with a fresh kerchief. He was smiling as he walked down the street towards the narrow, brick-built frontage of the sheriff's office.

The office had a solid-looking door on the right-hand side and a barred window on the left. There was a tall man slumped in a worn hickory rocker outside the door, his grey stetson tilted over his face and both heels up on the rail. His gunbelt was hiked over the spread of a widening gut, with the butt of a Remington Army model nudging the rolls of fat on the left side.

'Cobly,' said Stanton. 'You awake?'

'Sure.' The grey hat moved no more than the grey-haired head. 'What is it, Cole?'

38

'I want to swear out a warrant,' said Stanton. 'For murder.'

'Yeah?' Sheriff Vance Cobly swung his feet down from the rail and stood up. He was two good inches taller than Stanton. 'Fer who?'

'Billy Eagle.' Stanton hooked thumbs inside the pockets of his black vest. 'He just admitted killing two of my men.'

'Best come inside.' Cobly dragged a dirty white cuff over his face. 'Tell me in the office.'

The office was small, most of it taken up by the wide desk and the swivel chair. There was a pot-belly stove, unlit in the summer heat, against one wall and a rack of shotguns and Winchester carbines against the other. Behind the desk there was a door, open now, so that it gave a view of the two small cells occupying the rear of the building. The cells were fronted with solid steel bars, divided by more bars and wire mesh. There was a window at the rear, cut into the brickwork so that it spanned the partitioning bars to provide light for both cages. There were narrow bunks fixed against the walls, with slop pots under each bunk.

Cobly swung the door shut and sat down behind his desk. He gestured at the high-back chair facing it. Stanton sat down.

'You sure you want to do this, Cole?' Cobly swivelled his chair so that he could open a drawer. He took out a bottle of whiskey and filled two glasses. 'It looks a mite obvious.'

Stanton smiled. It looked like a tombstone splitting. He drank whiskey.

'I'm sure, Vance,' he said. 'I got solid evidence.'

'Tell me.'

Cobly set his glass down and hiked a pad towards

him. He licked the end of a pencil and stared at Stanton.

Stanton said: 'About a month ago I sent two of my boys into the Piñons. Donny and Osmond. They never come back.'

Scribbling notes, Cobly asked: 'Why's that, Cole. Why'd you send them?'

'It matter?' Stanton shrugged. 'I got a taste for deer meat. Donny was a good tracker. Osmond was a marksman.'

'You waited a long time to tell me,' said Cobly. 'How come?'

'Hell!' Stanton poured more whiskey without waiting for an invitation. 'I thought they were funning around. Taking time out to hunt. Until Billy showed up.'

'I heard he was in town again,' said Cobly, almost reluctantly. 'What's he got to do with it?'

'He's wearing one of Donny's pistols,' said Stanton. 'You know that matched pair? Well, Billy's got one on his hip and the other in his kit. He's over to the Little Sister right now, boasting how he killed two men and took a pair of guns. Says he didn't bother with Osmond's Sharps because he didn't need a gun like that.'

'Billy'd say most anythin' when he's likkered up,' warned Cobly.

Stanton's face got colder than normal. Like marble freezing. He put down his glass.

'You doubting my word, Vance?'

'No.' The big man said it fast; worried. 'I ain't doubtin' your word, Cole. I'm just sayin' folks might talk.'

'About a halfbreed?' Stanton picked up his glass again. 'With witnesses?'

'Who?' asked Cobly.

'Maggie Wills and Lindy Dalton,' said Stanton. 'They both heard the conversation. They'll testify it's the truth.'

'I bet they will,' murmured Cobly. 'You want me to arrest Billy?'

Stanton smiled: 'You want to stay sheriff of Chandler's Butte, Vance?'

Cobly shrugged and emptied his glass. 'I guess.'

'Then let's go.'

'Hold on.' Cobly waved his hands. 'Where's Billy now?'

'In the Little Sister,' said Stanton. 'I left him a bottle, so he won't have strayed far.'

'All right.' Sheriff Cobly stood up, hiking his gunbelt higher over his increasing gut. 'Let's go.'

Stanton chuckled and followed the big man out of the office.

Billy Eagle was in one of the rooms built out back of the saloon. There were five, each one equipped with a bed and a washstand. A towel. And a woman. Billy had two: he could afford them.

When Vance Cobly kicked the door open and walked through with the big Remington in his hand, Billy was curled up between Maggie and Lindy. He didn't even hear the door thud open until Maggie, who was slightly less occupied than Lindy, screamed.

'You're under arrest, Billy,' said the sheriff. 'Stand up.'

'He is!' shrieked Lindy. 'You bastard!'

She climbed clear of the pillows as Maggie vacated the end of the bed. Billy just grinned and licked his lips.

'Stand up,' repeated Cobly as the two women

dragged on their clothes. 'I got a warrant fer your arrest.'

Billy's stand disappeared fast. He wiped his mouth. 'Why? What I done?'

'Killed two men,' said Cobly. 'Said so in front of witnesses. Got one more to swear you're carryin' the guns of a dead man.'

'They was huntin' me,' Billy complained. 'Lookin' fer my gold.'

'You admitting it?' asked Cobly. 'You sayin' you killed Osmond and Donny?'

'They was tryin' to kill me,' said Billy. 'Sure I killed them. What else I do?'

'Get dressed,' said Cobly. 'Fast.'

Billy Eagle was locked up in the right-hand cell. Cole Stanton, Jimmy Witt and Art Durant swore depositions that identified the pearl-handled Colts as belonging to Donny. Stanton, Maggie Wills and Lindy Dalton swore further testimony that Billy had admitted killing both Donny and Osmond.

Sheriff Vance Cobly had no choice but to lock up the halfbreed until the circuit judge came round. He had a fair idea of what had happened, but there was too much sworn evidence against Billy for him to risk letting the man go free. And, besides, he knew that if he did, he would risk losing his post: Cole Stanton pulled sufficient strings to dump any Frontier lawman. So he locked Billy Eagle up and waited.

And while he waited, Cole Stanton got busy.

The tubercular man wired Phoenix to call in a specialist, a man he had used before. The man was called Joel Meek, though his name betrayed his nature. Meek was a good five inches over six feet, with a body to match. He looked like a grizzly bear: all hair and furious eyes. His waist was near as broad as his shoulders, with a LeMat holstered on the right hip and a Colt's Peacemaker with a cutaway guard on the left. He had been a slave-master at sixteen, on a plantation in Virginia. During the Civil War he had ridden with Quantrill. He was wanted in Missouri, Arkansas and the Oklahoma Territory. And he hated anyone who wasn't guaranteed pure white.

He came in on a S.A.W. stage, around mid-day one hot July afternoon.

By nightfall of the next day he had a crowd whipped up to take the jail and lynch Billy Eagle.

That was Joel Meek's main attribute: he had a way with crowds. He could talk up a storm and let the lash of his tongue carry the people along. And if they wanted a leader, then Joel Meek was out in front, ready to use the shotgun barrel of his LeMat against anyone who stood in his way.

Vance Cobly stood in his way.

The sheriff was a weak man. He knew that, at fifty, he was closing fast on the end of his career. That was why he had let Cole Stanton dictate most of his moves: the skeletal businessman had the money to keep a compliant peace officer in office.

Yet Cobly was still invested with a small degree of honour, and he felt it his duty to protect his prisoners until the circuit judge could get round to try them and hang them according to Stanton's wishes.

So he came out onto the sidewalk with a Remington scattergun in his hands and told the crowd to go away.

The crowd went on arguing that a dirty halfbreed like Billy Eagle should be hung right off. Joel Meek went on whipping them up. Until Cole Stanton gave him a signal and he calmed the crowd.

Vance Cobly wiped sweat from his brow as they dispersed. He wasn't sure why, but he was grateful. He knew that if he let a prisoner get taken from his jail he would lose his badge; knew, too, that if he didn't give Stanton his way, he would never get re-elected.

He turned as Stanton came up the sidewalk with a smile like a slit gut on his pale face.

'He must be pretty frightened by now.' Stanton clapped Cobly on the shoulder. 'With a mob ready to lynch him.'

'You planned all this?' Cobly lowered the hammers of the shot gun. 'I mighta been killed.'

'No.' Stanton shook his head. 'I planned it better than that.'

'How?' The sheriff stared into the evening, wiping sweat from his face. 'How you work that?'

'Listen,' said Stanton, 'listen good.'

Cobly nodded. 'All right, Cole. But I don't want another lynch mob.'

'You may need one,' said Stanton. 'To work it out.'

'I'll lose my badge if I hand a prisoner over.' Cobly eased his bulk against the warm brickwork of the jail, unpleasantly conscious of the sweat dripping down his back. 'The county seat'll take it away.'

'If my plan works, you won't need a badge.' Stanton reached inside his coat to produce a bottle of whiskey. 'You'll be rich if you listen to me.'

Cobly took the bottle and sucked hard and long on the neck.

'I don't want the 'breed killed,' said Stanton; softly. 'That would be stupid. I just want him scared. So scared he'll tell me – us – where he's got that Spanish gold cached. Jesus Christ! Think about it, Vance. He's bringing in around three thousand dollars' worth a month. Pure bars! He doesn't even know what they're worth. He's already picked up more money than he ever thought he'd make in nine lifetimes, and all he does is spend it on cheap whores and whiskey.'

'That you supply,' said Cobly. 'Don't forget that, Cole.'

'I'm not,' said Stanton. 'I'm in business to make a profit. I'm giving Billy what he wants, and now I can give you the same.'

'What's that, Cole?' The peace officer drank more whiskey. 'What is it that I want?'

'To quit?' said Stanton. 'Leave off your gun and take Elizabeth someplace where you don't need to walk around with a pistol on your hip? Not worry about some drunken cowboy shooting you in the back? Not face a lynch mob anymore?'

'I'd need money for that,' said Cobly. 'More than a peace officer's wages pay.'

'That's what I'm offering,' said Stanton. 'A chance. Look: if we can get that goddam halfbreed scared enough he'll tell us where from he fetches that gold. The way he's bringing it in, there's enough for all of us. Me, you, my men.'

'I took an oath,' said Cobly. 'I swore to keep the peace when I took this badge.'

'What's it pay you?' asked Stanton. 'Enough to quit this job and take your wife to St. Louis? Buy a house there? Enough to live comfortable for the rest of your lives?'

Cobly shook his head.

'That's what I'm offering you,' said the lean-faced man, speaking slow and sure; confident. 'A way out. An easy way out, with everything paid for.'

The lawman drank more whiskey and rubbed at his belly.

'What you want me to do, Cole?'

'Help me scare the shit clear of Billy's pants,' said Stanton. 'Get him so goddam frightened that all he wants to do is get clear of the jail and tell us where he's got the Spanish gold cached.'

'Suppose he won't?' asked the lawman. 'What then?'

'He's looking forward to the circuit judge coming round,' said Stanton. 'The kind of evidence against him, he don't stand a chance. He'll hang. He knows that : he'll tell. So long as he keeps on getting reminded.'

'Billy's tough,' said Cobly. 'He might just get himself hung without telling anyone.'

'So we let him go,' grinned Stanton. 'We work some kind of a jail break, and trail him back.'

'You tried that before,' said Cobly. 'It didn't work.'

'If he won't tell us,' replied Stanton, 'then he'll be running so scared there'll be trailers of shit to mark his path. All the way to the Spanish gold.'

'All right.' Cobly nodded. 'But I don't like treading in it.'

'What?' asked Stanton. 'The gold?'

'No,' said Cobly, emptying the bottle. 'The shit.'

CHAPTER FOUR

Azul rode into Chandler's Butte late one hot July afternoon.

The town was mostly quiet, except for a small group of men outside the jail house, and they weren't doing much except passing a jug of home brew around and mumbling about a lynching. The town was large for this part of the Arizona country. Mainstreet was wide and dusty, there was a windmill at one end, sucking water up into a catchment tank, and a peeling, white-painted church at the other. In between, there was The Hotel and the Little Sister saloon; a spread of stores selling hardware, saddle tack, dry goods and hats; a livery stable. There was a stage office and a bank; an assay office alongside the bank. The jail. Sand-packed alleys bled off either side of mainstreet, lined with small frame houses that boasted an alternation of gardens and smallholdings, according to the owners' taste and wealth.

Azul checked the grey stallion into the livery and slung his saddlebags on his shoulder as he walked down to The Hotel. He booked himself a room that cost a dollar a night with breakfast, and ordered a bath.

By the time he had soaked in the hot water, and scrubbed himself clean of trail dirt, it was getting dark. He went down to the restaurant attached to the hotel and ate beefsteak with pan-fried potatoes and greens. Then he went to the saloon.

47

The Little Sister was a single-storey adobe building with fly-blown windows both sides of the batwings. It was plank-floored, with sawdust spread over the wood and a long bar running down one side. There was a picture hung behind the bar, an enormous, garish depiction of a girl with gigantic breasts fondling the neck of a swan that had his head planted between her legs. Across the wide room, there was a mirror of the same size, reflecting the painting. There were round tables and low-backed chairs spaced down the room. At the end, where a door opened on the rear of the building, there was a roulette wheel and a table rolling Keno Goose. Five cowboys were laying bets on the spin of the wheel and losing money to the house. Two Mexicans were watching the Keno tumblers roll out. There were also two poker games going on.

Azul went up to the bar and ordered whiskey.

A bottle with no label got shoved in front of him, accompanied by a dirty glass. He filled the glass and took a long swallow. It was the first whiskey he had tasted since leaving Billy Eagle. It went down hot and sour.

He filled a second glass and took it slower. It tasted better. He filled a third.

'Ain't that just the way?' The voice was hoarse with liquor. 'Let one halfbreed in an' they all think they got a right to drink alongside white folks.'

Azul turned to face the man. He was big: well over six feet, topping Azul by at least three inches, with a bristling black beard covering most of his face.

'Jesus!' he said. 'I had my way, there wouldn't be a red nigger brat let into a decent saloon. Better still, there wouldn't be one left alive.'

Azul set his glass down. Casually. Carefully.

'You got some objection?' he asked. 'To me drinking here?'

'Yeah.' The big man nodded. 'I object to standing in a saloon with a goddam fuckin' halfbreed. I don't like the idea of drinking out of a glass some squawman's spillin' used.'

Azul stared at the man, letting his eyes wander over the massive hulk to take in the scene beyond.

He remembered something his father had told him, the first time he ever visited a saloon. It was in a town called Huatachi.

Kieron Gunn had said : *'You got as much right to drink as any man, so long as you got the money to pay for it. Anyone tries to stop you, you tell him that. If he keeps on arguing, then you try to explain it to him.'*

Azul had asked his father, *'Why?'*

'Every man deserves an explanation,' Kieron had said. *'If he don't accept it, then you need to work it out between you. But don't back down.'*

There were two men behind the big man. One was red-haired and almost as large; with a shotgun cradled in his arms. The other was thin and fancy under a frilly shirt and two S & W Schofields. They were both standing up from the table, watching the scene at the bar.

'I paid for it,' said Azul. 'Why shouldn't I drink it?'

'Because you're a squawman's brat,' said the big man. 'Because I don't like ass droppings from hot-legged injun bitches.'

Raw, red rage possessed Azul. He swung his hand around, still holding the glass. As it hit the big man's face, he cupped his hand, driving the heel of his palm hard against the base as the rim shattered over Joel Meek's nose and mouth.

The glass broke on the teeth and the angle of the nose. The rim fragmented, shards flying clear of the face as more dug into the beard and mustache. Joel Meek screamed. Blood gusted from his face; more came from his cut gums. He opened his arms and reached for the halfbreed.

Azul moved back, lifting a foot up in a high kick that angled his toe against the big man's genitals. At the same time, he drew his Colt to cover the men across the room.

Meek went down on his knees, spitting blood.

And something hard and heavy rammed into Azul's back.

'Drop the gun!'

The barkeep's voice was whiney, but the double *click!* of the twin hammers going back was unmistakeable. Azul lowered the hammer of the Colt and turned to set the revolver on the bar.

'All right,' said the 'keep. 'Now set to.'

As Joel Meek came up off the floor Azul kicked him in the mouth. The big man grunted and rolled back. Azul was moving towards him when two feet, clad in high-heeled boots, slammed against his knees, tumbling him over and down onto the sawdust. Abruptly, like a new-found mountain erupting from the ground, Meek was up on his knees with his hands clasped together to drive against Azul's face.

The halfbreed rolled, taking the blow on his left shoulder. He grabbed the clenched hands and dragged them towards him, turning the big man on his side as he brought his legs up to smash both feet against Meek's stomach.

It was like kicking an iron wall. Meek just laughed and pulled his hands away.

Azul stood up.

Meek rose, grinning. He spread his arms.

Azul waited until they were closing on his chest, then reached forwards to sink his fingers into Meek's beard. At the same time, he lifted his left leg to plant the sole against Meek's belly and folded his right. He went down on his back, hauling the bigger man over the pivot of his foot to crash a yard behind him as he let loose his grip.

Meek yelled and broke more teeth on the floor. Azul twisted round to slam both feet against the giant's back. Meek groaned. And a second later, Azul was on his feet again.

He waited until the hairy man was lifting off the floor, then kicked him twice. Once in the chest, the second time in the belly.

Joel Meek doubled over, groaning. Azul kicked him in the side, and then again at the base of the neck. Meek went limp.

And Vance Cobly came in through the batwings with a scattergun in his hands and a dutiful expression on his face.

'What's goin' down here?' he asked. 'Levy?'

The barkeep shrugged. 'Joel made some comments, Vance. The halfbreed took exception. Picked a fight. Christ! He's kicked the shit outta Joel.'

'All right.' Cobly turned the shotgun to point on Azul. 'You best come with me.'

'I didn't start it,' said the halfbreed. 'I was just taking a drink.'

'I heard that before,' said Cobly. 'Walk out slow.'

Azul looked at the dark holes the shotgun was pointing at his belly and shrugged. Cobly rammed the muzzles up against him and reached over his grip to take the Colt from the bar. He tucked the pistol into his belt.

'All right, Mister. Walk out slow.'

Azul went out with his hands in the air and hate in his heart. He paced down the sidewalk with Cobly's shotgun jamming against his ribs.

They reached the jail and Cobly kicked the door open. Azul went through. The sheriff opened the rearwards door and nudged Azul into the corridor. He reached over to spin the key and swing the barred door open, then kicked the halfbreed through and swung the door shut with a practised movement.

The key closed in the lock.

'You get fed twice a day,' he said. 'Until the circuit judge arrives. Keep quiet, an' keep your cell clean, else you don't get fed.'

Without waiting for an answer he closed the outer door and the cells got dark.

Azul checked the confines of the cage. The bunk was narrow and mattressed with a plain, hard palliasse. The walls on two sides were solid brick, on the others, steel bars and wire mesh where the cells divided. The floors and roofs were solid.

Azul went up to the mesh of wire dividing his cell from the next and rattled it against the bars.

The man slumped on the bunk beyond woke up, rubbing an irritable hand over his whiskey-rimmed eyes.

He sat up, shaking his head. He spat on the floor, then looked at Azul.

'*Jesus Cristo!* You!'

Azul looked at Billy Eagle and said, 'Yeah. Me.'

'What they get you for?' asked Billy.

'They don't seem to like halfbreeds here,' said Azul. 'Someone picked a fight in the saloon. Why they got you?'

Billy Eagle shrugged. 'I thought you might be trailin' me, so I doubled back. I took them fancy guns the black-haired kid was using. They got me on murder.'

'Seem's like we both have to wait,' said Azul. 'I beat up a man in the saloon.'

'What he look like?' asked Billy. 'Tell me.'

Azul described Joel Meek.

'One from Stanton,' said Billy. 'That bastard's fixing to take my gold. Donny and Osmond were his men. Now he's brought in another: Joel Meek. Stanton figgers to scare me out.'

'What'll you do?' asked Azul.

'Nothing,' said Billy. 'They got me in here on a murder charge. Say I killed Osmond and Donny. But they won't hang me until Cole Stanton finds out where I got the gold hid. They gotta keep me alive for that.'

'Congratulations,' said Azul. 'How you figure my chances.'

Billy Eagle shrugged: 'I don't know. Cole Stanton's the biggest man around here, so he does what he wants, pretty much. It's kinda funny that you didn't get killed straight off; messing into one of his men.'

'Thanks,' said Azul. 'Thanks a lot. That really makes me feel better.'

'Friend,' said Billy Eagle, 'it should. The way folks around Chandler's Butte feel about halfbreeds, you're lucky to be alive.'

'I'm not,' said Azul. 'Not inside a cell.'

'There's a way out,' said Billy, pointing at the gallows behind the jail. 'A short walk and a long drop.'

CHAPTER FIVE

Azul was surprised when he got taken out the cell the next morning.

A big man with red hair and a cut-down scatter-gun on a sling-strap over his wide shoulder supervised the event, accompanied by a slender man with a fancy, frill-fronted shirt and two S & W Schofields. The peace officer stood aside as they led him out of the jail, pretending not to see what was happening.

Azul got walked down the street to The Hotel. In through a rear door and up a short flight of stairs to the first and only level.

The red-head shoved him through the door while the man in the frilly shirt kept a Schofield cocked against the small of his back. The door slammed shut with the red-head outside and the S & W still planted tight against his spine.

The room was large. Two windows were open against the far wall, shutters adjusted to let in air without too much sunlight. There was a soft carpet on the floor and a table at the centre. Three chairs, high-backed and leather-covered, were set around the table. There were paintings on the walls. There was a decanter in the middle of the table, with three glasses.

Two men came out of a second room.

One was the man Azul had fought the night before. He had bandages on his face, and he looked angry. The other man was very tall and very thin, with a face like a smiling tombstone, and a black suit like an undertaker's.

He smiled like an empty skull welcoming a man into hell, and said: 'My name is Cole Stanton. What shall I call you?'

Azul shrugged, and said: 'Azul.'

'Sit down,' said Stanton. 'Please.'

The man in the frilly shirt backed up against the door with the S & W Schofield canted inside his left elbow. The bandaged giant sat down at the table. Azul sat down.

Stanton filled the three glasses, then sat down himself.

'It's very good liquor,' he said. 'Imported. Whisky, without the *e*.'

He drank some, wiping his mouth afterwards with a silk kerchief. Azul lifted his glass and sipped the liquor. It was as good as Stanton had promised: clean and cool until it hit, then lazily warm.

'Why?' he asked. 'Why did you bring me here?'

'I have a proposition,' said Stanton. 'One that could make us a lot of money.'

Azul sipped more of the imported whisky.

'What?'

'You're charged with assault.' Stanton gestured at the sullen face of Joel Meek. 'The way this town feels about halfbreeds right now, that could see you lynched. At best, Vance Cobly will keep you in the jail until the circuit judge arrives. That could be a month from now, maybe more. You want to stay locked up so long?'

Azul shook his head.

'Good,' said Stanton. 'I think we understand one another.'

56

'You can't trust a 'breed,' rumbled Meek. 'They're born liars.'

Stanton turned his face on the giant and Meek went quiet.

'I want you to talk with Billy Eagle,' said Stanton. 'Real close. Get him to tell you where he's fetching that old gold from. I'll pay you one thousand dollars or one percent, whichever's highest. He'll talk to one of his own kind, especially in jail.'

Azul sipped whisky. 'Why not take him out? Talk to him direct?'

'It wouldn't work.' Stanton shook his head. 'Billy's stubborn.'

Azul nodded in the direction of Joel Meek, then pointed a thumb over his shoulder at the man behind him. 'You got persuasion.'

'No.' Stanton shook his head again. 'He'd die before he told me. Besides, he could lie. It needs doing carefully. Which is a lucky break for you.'

'I'll still be in jail,' murmured Azul, emptying his glass. 'That's lucky?'

Stanton lifted the stopper on the decanter and tilted the crystal over the halfbreed's glass. The facets sent multicoloured rays of sparkling light over his hand.

'You agree to help me,' said Stanton, 'I'll get you out. You find out what I want to know, then I get you set free – Joel here will drop all charges. You also get a cut.'

He smiled as Azul raised the glass and took a long swallow. 'Well?'

Azul grinned cynically. It was ironic that his saving of Billy Eagle's life had resulted in the halfbreed getting thrown into jail on a murder charge of which he was innocent. Ironic, too, that the real killer was now given a chance to go free: if he would betray Billy Eagle. He felt little doubt that if he agreed, Stanton would leave Billy to hang. Most likely arrange Azul's death, too.

'What happens to Billy?' he asked. 'After.'

'You care?' Stanton shrugged.

Azul went on staring at the hollow-cheeked man without speaking. Finally Stanton dabbed at his mouth and said, 'He'll have to die. There's no other way.'

Azul emptied his glass and set it down on the table. His blue eyes bored into Stanton's face. They were very cold. He smiled without any humour showing, and when he spoke his voice was very clear.

'Go to hell.'

Stanton sighed: a businessman confronted with a temporary setback. He stoppered the decanter and carried it over to a glass-fronted armoire. Opened the cupboard and set the crystal carefully inside. He came back to the table and picked up the glasses. Shut them behind the carefully-bevelled panes.

'You're making a foolish mistake.'

Azul shrugged.

'All right.' Stanton turned to Joel Meek, 'Persuade him.'

The giant climbed to his feet. It was impossible to see whether or not he was smiling behind the bandages, but his small, piggy eyes had an evil glint.

'Here?' he asked.

'No.' Stanton's kerchief fluttered as he frowned. 'Take him out back. And Joel, I don't want him killed. Or crippled. Just persuaded.'

Meek grunted. Like a boar driven off a particularly tasty meal.

'Remember that, Joel,' warned the black-clad man. 'I want him alive and useful.'

Azul set his feet flat on the carpet, hands gripping the edge of the table. It was a long chance, but if he could turn the table against the giant and ram the chair into the fancy-dressed man behind him, he might just have a chance. Then the cold muzzle of the S & W touched his neck just under his right ear, and a soft voice said, 'Don't try it. I'd hate to blow a pretty face like yours apart.'

Azul froze. Meek came around the table. He sank a hand into Azul's shirtfront and hauled the half-breed upright. 'I'm gonna enjoy this,' he grunted.

The LeMat came out of the holster, the massive pistol looking normal size in his giant paw. He cocked the gun and drove the muzzle hard into Azul's stomach.

'Let's go.'

He released his grip on Azul's shirt and spun the halfbreed round. The thin man with the frilly shirt walked backwards to the door. Opened it. Meek pushed Azul through.

Outside, the red-head with the cut-down shotgun grinned. 'Well?'

'He don't like the idea.' It was the man in the fancy shirt who spoke, his voice pitched up high with anticipatory excitement. 'Needs persuadin'.'

The red-head sniffed and scratched at his beard : 'Fine.'

They walked Azul to the end of the corridor, where a narrow door opened onto a flight of narrow stairs that went down to the yard behind the hotel. There was a rear porch lined with empty barrels and piled with garbage. In a fenced-off section, pigs rooted at the ground. A high picket fence surrounded the yard. There was a dilapidated shed at the far end. They went inside.

It was gloomy, the only light coming from the

holes in the roof. A few bales of mouldering straw were stacked at the far end and the walls were hung with pieces of discarded tack that no one had got around to throwing out. Joel Meek planted one hand against Azul's back and sent the halfbreed staggering forwards. He crashed against one of the posts supporting the roof and spun away, fighting to retain his balance.

'All right.' Meek unstrapped his gunbelt and hung it on a nail. 'Let's do it.'

'Wait!' The man in the frilly shirt licked his lips, his dark eyes gleaming. 'Undress first.'

'Christ!' Meek grumbled. 'Don't you ever get enough, Art?'

The man tittered. 'No.'

Meek shrugged: 'Do it, you goddam squaw dropping.'

Azul removed his clothes. The man called Art giggled. 'Well hung, ain't he, Joel?'

'Shut yore mouth.' Meek hiked his thumbs into his pant's top, staring at Azul. 'My name's Joel Meek,' he said. 'I hate injuns. This is Art Durant: he likes a well-built man. Him,' he pointed at the red-headed man. 'He's Jimmy Witt.'

'I'll remember the names,' said Azul. 'Need to, for the markers.'

Jimmy Witt guffawed. 'He's real spunky, Joel.'

'I bet,' said Art Durant, staring at Azul's groin. 'I just bet he is.'

'He's trash,' snarled Meek. 'Red nigger trash! A decent man wouldn't touch filth like that.'

Durant shrugged, reluctantly taking his eyes from Azul's crotch.

'Grab him,' ordered Meek. 'Hold him.'

Jimmy Witt stepped forwards with the scattergun

pointed on Azul's belly. He moved round to the side until he was in position to take hold of the right arm. Then Art Durant stepped over to take the left. They lowered their guns, holding Azul by his wrists and biceps, twisting his arms viciously up his back.

Joel Meek came up close. His bandages puckered as he spat into Azul's face, leaving a gobbet of crimson-tinted phlegm running down the halfbreed's cheek. Azul kicked out, trying to land a foot in the giant's groin. Meek laughed, moving out of range. Then he stepped forwards again and landed an open-handed slap against Azul's cheek.

It was like getting hit with a side of wood. Azul's head jumped sideways as fire sprang over his face. The left hand came up to strike against the other cheek. Lights danced over the halfbreed's eyes. Meek reached over his shoulder to grab the long, blond hair. He tugged it tight, hauling Azul's head back. Then began to slap.

It was like burning brands on Azul's face. He felt sweat burst from his forehead. Felt his teeth rattle in his mouth. His eyes watered, and a thin trickle of moisture ran from his nose.

Then he felt his head let go and saw Joel Meek's enormous fist coming up like an approaching locomotive. It landed between his eyes and an enormous burst of light spread over his mind, sparking lances of red fire across his eyes so that they closed as a thick wave of ultimate darkness blanked out his vision.

The darkness went away as pain exploded upwards from his groin. He groaned, feeling spittle fall from his mouth as the agony roiled through his belly and his throat filled with vomit.

Witt and Durant held him upright as his legs lifted in automatic reaction to the pain, and he gagged, spitting puke down his chest. There was a pause then, just long enough for him to clear his throat and get his eyes open again. And then the huge fists began to slam against his stomach.

He urinated, causing a second pause in the beating as Meek jumped back from the yellow flood. It lasted only a few seconds, and the fists began to pound again, thudding against his stomach and ribs. Waves of red light washed over his eyes, interspersed with dancing candles of yellow pain. He twisted, but Durant and Witt held too tight a grip, so that all he did was present his sides to Meek's fists.

And after a while there was a darkness so black that it covered all the light and he went down into it with what felt like a grateful sigh.

He woke with something cold on his face. Opened his eyes and mouth. Closed them as the water filled the orbs and spilled into his mouth, choking him.

'He's awake,' said Art Durant.

'Good,' said Joel Meek. 'Turn him over on those bales.'

'I ain't goin' fer that,' protested Jimmy Witt. 'Not that stuff.'

Durant giggled.

'Do it,' snarled Meek. 'Now!'

They dragged Azul to his feet and carried him, stumbling, over to the straw. They shoved him face down, lifted on his toes as they spread his arms and held him in position. Meek picked up a chunk of flat, worm-eaten boarding.

'Hold him there.'

He stepped up beside Azul, raising the plank in both hands. Then he brought it down over the half-breed's naked buttocks. Azul jerked, his face grinding into the straw. He felt the long, soggy shafts between his teeth and bit on them as the plank landed again and again. His hair got thick with sweat, and tears rolled reluctantly from his eyes. His buttocks were on fire, and each blow slammed his belly against the rough edges of the bales, sparking nausea from deep inside his gut.

He closed his eyes, forcing his mind away from the pain, back to a better time. A time spent with the Chiricahua, high up in the Mogallons.

Living can be pain, Old Sees-The-Fox had told him. *How can a man appreciate happiness without sadness to make the other side of the coin? How can he know comfort unless he also knows pain?*

The important thing is to understand it, and to control it. A warrior who suffers pain shows his courage. To die is an easy thing. A bullet, a lance, a knife —they can end life with little suffering. To endure pain and come out on the other side, that is a mark of real courage. A true warrior accepts that. Accepts the pain. He dies with his mouth closed, or lives to return the suffering.

Remember that, boy.

Azul clamped his teeth tighter on the mouldy straw and felt the agony fade away into a single numbing ache that seemed to consume his entire body until a great looming blackness like a winter's night with a storm blowing up enfolded him and took him away to a very quiet place where there was nothing but warmth and darkness.

He came out of the blackness with great reluctance. It was warm and safe down there. There was no pain, no danger : only nothingness. But then something else intruded : hate. It climbed up from the pain-numbed recesses of his mind. It was like the single

63

glowing coal at the centre of a hogan's night-fire. Dully smouldering until blown on, when it glowed afresh and sent little trailers of flame over the fresh twigs, sparking them into life so that they began to burn and then to blaze. Azul nursed the little fire, stoking it with his mind until it got greater and began to roar through his body.

Joel Meek.

Art Durant.

Jimmy Witt.

Cole Stanton.

They were the fuel that stoked the fire of hatred. They were the ones who must die.

He opened his eyes.

The shed was dark, except for a single lantern burning at the centre. Jimmy Witt was hunkered down on the straw with a half-rolled cigarette in his hand. Joel Meek and Art Durant were just outside the pale glow. They were very close, and Meek was moaning softly as Durant touched him.

'He's awake.' Witt sounded grateful for the interruption. 'He's comin' round.'

Meek and Durant stood up, keeping their backs turned as they fumbled with their clothing.

Azul spat blood and rolled onto his side. His body hurt.

'You changed yore mind yet?' asked Meek. 'You wanna do what Cole said?'

Azul started to nod, but the motion set his head spinning.

'Yeah,' he mumbled, conscious of the thickness of his words. 'I'll do it.'

'Good,' said Meek. 'Get dressed.'

They had to help him into his clothes, and then support him as they carried him back to the hotel.

'I thought you'd see sense,' said Stanton. 'You never really had any other choice.'

'No,' said Azul slowly. 'I guess not.'

'When you go back,' said Stanton, 'tell Billy you got beaten up. Tell him I arranged it. That should put you on his side better than anything. When you've got something to tell me, ask Cobly for a doctor. Say you hurt from the beating. Cobly will arrange for you to come out. Then you tell me.'

'Suppose Billy won't talk?' asked Azul. 'What then?'

'Give it a week,' said Stanton. 'If he hasn't talked by then, ask for the doctor anyway. I'll think of something else.'

Azul nodded, adding a fifth name to his list: Vance Cobly.

'All right,' said Stanton. 'Take him back.'

This time they were more gentle. Durant and Witt held him upright as Meek led the way down the street. Cobly looked at his face as they entered the jail and opened the cell without speaking. The bars clanged shut and the outer door closed. A small lantern burned on a shelf in the narrow corridor outside the cells.

Azul eased slowly onto his bunk. His stomach was aching and his buttocks felt raw. He stretched on his side, trying to find a soft spot in the palliasse to accommodate his bruised face.

'*Madre de Dios!*' Billy Eagle came up to the intervening mesh. 'What did they do to you?'

Azul grunted.

'Who was it?' asked Billy. 'Stanton's men?'

'Yeah.' Azul eased clear of the bunk without letting his buttocks touch. 'Joel Meek. Art Durant.

65

Jimmy Witt. Cobly knew about it.'

'*Cristo!*' Billy shook his head. 'They really worked you over.'

'Your fault.' Azul spat blood on the floor. 'They want me to talk to you.'

Billy laughed. 'About the mine? I'm not telling anyone.'

'Stanton offered me a thousand,' said Azul. 'To get the information. That, and my release.'

'And when I don't tell you?' said Billy. 'What then?'

'He'll think of something else,' murmured Azul. 'I reckon he'll break you out and hope to trail you.'

'I lost 'em before,' grunted Billy. 'I can do it again.'

'Reckon next time he'll have a whole posse on your tail,' said Azul. 'Keep you running so fast you don't get time to spit.'

'Why you tellin' me all this?' asked Billy. 'What for?'

'I want to get out of here,' said Azul. 'Way things are now, we both trail our heels until the circuit judge comes round. Then you get hung and I get sent to the penitentiary. Or Stanton has me killed.'

Billy Eagle swallowed hard. 'I'm bored in here,' he said slowly; cautiously. 'I got whisky up in the cave.'

He turned away from the bars, staring down at his moccasins, then up at the moonlight coming in through the window.

'Suppose we both get out?'

'Only way to do that is through Stanton,' said Azul. 'He's got a system worked out for me to tell him what you said about the mine.'

'An' you think he'll break us both out if I don't tell you?' queried Billy. 'So we can get free?'

'He'll follow,' said Azul. 'He's too goddam greedy to let it go. But I think I got a way.'

66

'Why should I trust you?' asked Billy. 'You could be lying.'

'What time is it?' Azul asked.

Billy shrugged. 'I ain't sure. Midnight?'

'When'd I get taken out?' Azul said.

'Before noon,' answered Billy. 'Not long after dawn, I guess.'

'They been beating me most of that time,' said Azul. 'I want the men who did that. I'm going to kill them. Stanton and Cobly, too.'

Billy Eagle stared back at the moon. It was lifting up over the sky, very full, with a great pale face that hung yellow against the sky.

'All right,' he said at last. 'You work it. Get us bust out of here. You get me clear, I'll cut you in.'

Azul shook his head. 'I don't want paying. I just want Stanton and his men.'

'I'll buy your bullets,' said Billy Eagle.

'You got a deal,' said Azul. 'A week or so from now, we'll be out.'

He went back to the bunk and eased slowly down onto the hard mattress. He felt very tired. But also satisfied. In a week, Stanton should be worrying, and then he could lure the man into his second mistake.

The first – the way Azul reckoned it – was having him beaten up. The way the halfbreed saw the situation, that had established a blood debt that could only be settled in blood.

It was a satisfying thought.

CHAPTER SIX

The week passed slowly.

The food improved – presumably because Stanton wanted both men healthy – and Billy was allowed to buy in whiskey. The aches of Azul's beating faded slowly, though there remained heavy bruising on his stomach and over his buttocks. The crowd in front of the jail drifted away as Stanton eased off the pressure, and Chandler's Butte settled back into its normal routine.

It was Sunday morning, with the single bell mounted in the peeling white-washed tower of the church clanging a summons to the faithful, that Azul put his plan into action.

It was a high, bright morning. The sun was shining into the cells and the sky outside was a pure blue, uncluttered by clouds. The wood of the gallows behind the jail shone bright in the sun. The air was warm, heavy with the scent of juniper drifting down from the hills.

Azul rattled the bars of his cell and yelled for Cobly.

The sheriff came back into the corridor with a yawn on his face and a Sunday cigar in his mouth.

Azul clutched his stomach and kicked his unfinished breakfast out through the underhang of the door.

'I need a doctor,' he said. 'I'm bleeding inside.'

Cobly glanced at Billy Eagle, stretched out on his bunk with stertorian snores erupting like farts from his nose.

'All right. Wait.'

He went out through the adjoining door. Came back with the keys. Azul went on groaning and holding his belly as the door opened. Cobly angled the Remington on his face and took him out to the front office. He snapped cuffs over Azul's wrists and motioned the halfbreed onto the sidewalk.

Mainstreet was empty. From inside the church there came the sound of hymning.

Let the water and the blood ...

Hide myself in Thee ...

A big yellow dog snarled as Cobly's boots rang on the silent boardwalk. It bared its teeth and backed under the porch, dragging a half-chewed hunk of bone with it. Cobly spat on the tip of the cigar and tucked it inside his vest. Azul stood upright and let the sheriff guide him down the street.

They reached The Hotel and went in the back way.

Stanton was in his room. He had a dark blue dressing gown on, the silken material interlaid with patterns of green dragons.

'Well?' he asked.

Azul lifted his wrists: 'Want to take these off?'

Stanton nodded and Cobly produced the key.

Azul sat down.

'Well?' repeated Stanton. 'What is it?'

'Billy won't tell me where the mine is,' said Azul. 'But I got him persuaded I can organise a jail break.'

'How?' asked Stanton; cautious.

'It matter?' asked Azul. 'He's ready to go. He's scared of dying, so he'll take any chance he can.'

Stanton looked at Cobly.

The sheriff said, 'Powder could break the bars. It'd hafta to be something like that.'

Stanton nodded. 'Yes. We'd need to plan it care-

fully. My men can't do it: that'd be too obvious.'
He turned to Azul. 'Would your Indian friends do
it?'

Azul shook his head. 'Not that way. They might
attack the town, or they might sneak something in to
me. Not powder.'

'All right.' Stanton smiled. 'How does this sound?
I'll slip you a gun. Vance brings your food in and you
make him open the cell. We'll keep the town quiet
so you can get to the stable. I'll have your horse ready
with all your gear. Billy's too. I'll leave a stash of
flour in your bags, so you can mark the trail.'

'Sounds good,' said Azul. 'When?'

'Day after tomorrow,' said Stanton. 'Tuesday.'

Azul nodded.

'Remember one thing,' said Stanton. 'You try to
cross me and your life won't be worth a trodden
down dog turd.'

Azul smiled and nodded again.

Cobly took him back to the jail. Locked the door.

'Well?' asked Billy Eagle. 'When?'

'Day after tomorrow,' said Azul. 'Tuesday.'

Faintly, like a memory, the sound of a new hymn
drifted down the street.

'Amazing grace, how the sweet the sound
'That saved a wretch like me.
'I once was lost, but now I'm found . . .'

Azul slumped on the bunk and went to sleep.

Tuesday.

Bright and sunny. The air like warm buttermilk.
Lazy and hot; soothing.

Azul picked up his breakfast: two pan-fried eggs
and a mess of hash browns. He ate it all, then drank
the bitter coffee.

'Fer chrisakes!' whispered Billy Eagle. 'When we do it?'

Azul set his plate down and reached under the mattress to produce the Colt Stanton had slipped through the window the night before. It was – as he had expected – empty.

'Soon,' he said. 'Wait.'

Billy tipped the last of his whisky into his coffee and downed the mug in one long swallow.

'Ain't soon enough.'

Azul picked up his plate and rattled it against the bars. After a while the outer door opened and Vance Cobly came through. He faked surprise as Azul pointed the Colt through bars and said, 'Open the door.'

Cobly nodded and produced the keys, raising his hands as the halfbreed backed him against the wall and opened Billy Eagle's cell. Azul prodded him out into the main office. It was empty. From down the street there was the sound of music: a piano and banjos, striking a discordant rhythm.

'Stanton's got a church-building party goin' on,' said Cobly. 'Everyone's there.'

'Fine,' said Azul. 'Sit down.'

Cobly sat down.

Azul went over to the gun rack on the wall and took from it his belt. He buckled it on. Then he picked up his throwing knife and tucked it back inside his moccasin. Billy Eagle fastened his own belt around his waist and lifted a Colt's Peacemaker with a plain wood grip from the rack.

'I don't like them fancy guns no more,' he said. 'They just bring trouble.'

'Yeah,' said Azul.

And lifted the empty Colt from the desk to bring it round in a short, sharp arc that ended along the side of Vance Cobly's skull.

The sheriff's eyes burst open, then closed. He slumped down in the chair, his long arms dragging to the floor as his feet went out under the desk. A big purple bruise spread over his temple, getting lost in his thinning grey hair.

'Let's go,' said Azul. 'Fast.'

They crossed the street at a run, cutting through the back alleys to the stable.

The livery was empty except for the horses. Azul saddled the big grey stallion while Billy tacked up the bay gelding. Both men's Winchesters were in place. Both loaded. Only Billy's money was missing.

'Stanton thinks of everything,' he rasped. 'Don't he?'

'Not everything,' said Azul. 'He don't think we're riding free.'

He reached into his saddlebags to lift the flour sack out. Tossed it across the stable. It burst in a scattering cloud of white powder.

'Let's get,' he shouted; laughing.

They walked the horses out of the stable, cutting past the corrals behind rather than chancing mainstreet. From behind them came the tinkling of the piano and the twang of the banjos. The tune was *Virginia's Reel*. They walked past the small frame and adobe houses until they reached the outskirts of Chandler's Butte, where scrubby little gardens with pigs and goats rooting through them looked up with incurious eyes at their passing. Then Azul slammed his heels against the flanks of the grey and Billy Eagle whooped up the bay, and they took off at a fast gallop that headed them out through the dusty flatlands towards the distant foothills of the Piñon Llanos range.

72

They rode at that pace for close on ten miles, then slowed the horses to an easy canter that carried them over the parched scrub country to the more verdant lines of the mountain range.

Around noon they halted, turned the horses inside the shadow of a stand of scrub oaks. They were higher there than Chandler's Butte, and they could see the town easily. There was a thin column of dust spreading out, rising from around and behind the tiny black dots of mounted men.

'About six,' said Billy. 'What you reckon?'

'Six,' replied Azul. 'Coming hard.'

'We can lose 'em,' said Billy. 'Easy.'

'I don't want to lose them,' said Azul, his voice cold. 'They owe me.'

'Stanton won't chance all his men in one throw,' said Billy. 'He'll maybe send one out in front of a posse, but he'll keep the others back.'

'Let's find out,' rasped the halfbreed. 'Let's see who's there.'

'Sure.' Billy grinned. '*Enjuh!*'

'*Enjuh.*' Azul replied, in the Apache tongue. 'Good.'

They went on into the Piñon Llanos, drifting deliberately slow through the folds of oak and cottonwood and cedar. Leaving a clear trail, not hurrying. The foothills began to turn into real mountains as the day got darker. Canyons cut across the trail, heavy with the silver glow of the cottonwoods, dark with the leaves of the oaks. Wide spreads of shale turned the path upwards. High-standing pines shaded their passage, and the air was loud with birdsong.

They reached a place where twin walls of pine-clad rock gave way to a mountain meadow enfolded on all sides by steep slopes of grass and timber. The facing slope was sheer, the only entrance via the trail. They tethered their horses inside the meadow, leaving the animals to crop the grass as they ran back with rifles in their hands to the head of the trail.

The sun was beginning to fade behind the distant rimrock, spreading a clear golden glow over the menacingly tranquil scene. Azul took up position on one side of the cut, Billy Eagle on the other.

'Stanton's men are mine,' called Azul. 'Remember that.'

'You're greedy,' answered Billy. 'Don't hog 'em.'

'I'm not,' said Azul. 'Just rooting them out.'

CHAPTER SEVEN

For a long time after the sun went down torches flickered on the lower slopes, moving steadily upwards. Azul watched them in silence until the movement halted and the steady, motionless glow of a fire replaced the brands.

'It could be a trick,' he called softly. 'They could be working round behind us.'

'Ain't but this one trail up,' replied Billy. 'Any other way's gonna take them a full night's ride. Why don't we head out?'

'They'll keep on coming,' said Azul. 'Stanton must be mad enough now. Best we take them here.'

'I guess.' Billy yawned. 'Wish I had me a bottle.'

Azul said nothing. He turned on his side, head rested on his left arm. Very quickly he was asleep. It was a light sleep : a warrior's rest. His ears remained tuned to the sounds around him, and he knew that any unusual noise would bring him to instant wakefulness.

When he opened his eyes again there was mist shading through the timber. The dark blue-black of the night sky was replaced with grey, and off to the east a faint glow showed below the horizon. He sat up, shaking dew from his hair, rubbing the moisture over his face. He drank from his canteen and crossed the head of the cut to wake Billy Eagle.

'It's nearly dawn,' he said. 'They'll be coming soon.'

Billy sat up, rubbing at his eyes. He stretched, kneading his shoulders. Then he climbed stiffly to his feet and began to stamp around.

'I'm gettin' soft,' he grumbled. 'Too much high livin'. Christ! I could use a drink.'

Azul stared at him, seeing the effects cheap liquor had worked on his system. It was not uncommon. Before the *pinda-lick-oyi* penetrated the mountains of Apacheria, the tribes had brewed their own spirit, a fierce concoction called *tiswin*. Sometimes they would trade for – or take in a raid – tequila, or the weaker pulque, but such hard liquor as whiskey was unknown. And the *pinda-lick-oyi* traders had seen that, and seen in the absence, a profit that they exploited to its limits. Some Apaches could take the stuff, get drunk, and then forget it. Goklya – the war leader the whites knew as Geronimo – was a prodigious drinker. When he had access. Others became dependant on the rot-gut brew, sometimes dying as a result, more often trading their honour and choosing to live around the posts, or on the reservations, eking out a miserable living that gave them just enough to purchase whiskey at inflated prices. For halfbreeds it was often worse. Belonging fully to neither race, they felt like outcasts, and the bottle offered a comfort. Billy looked like one of these.

Azul shrugged, moving back to his own position. He felt no particular kinship with Billy Eagle, other than their shared hardships, but their destinies appeared to be linked. Stanton was clearly determined to take over Billy's find, and the cadaverous whiteman had earned Azul's enmity. Staying close to Billy seemed like the best way of drawing Stanton's men out, away from the protection of the town. That was why he had chosen not to kill Vance Cobly when he had the chance. To have killed the sheriff in his own jail would have meant a warrant being taken out against him. And with a dead peace officer on his record, Federal Marshals might have taken up his trail. He was already wanted in some states, and that afforded him enough trouble without adding the dogged pursuit of Federal lawmen to his problems.

No, he decided. This way was better. Draw Stanton's men out and whittle them down. Kill Cobly if he was with the posse. If not, then find some other way to even the score.

With typically Apache logic he dismissed such future possibilities and concentrated on the immediate problem.

He moved out to the edge of the cut as the first birds began to sing and the sun lifted over the far horizon. Thrushes and orioles and blackbirds set up a trilling that filled the air with music. The sun broke through the mist and filled the eastern sky with golden light. The grey that had clouded the heavens faded like rain water drying off a slate, and the sky got a clear, perfect blue. Mare's tails of white cloud showed high up, drifting on the wind. The dew-fresh trees gave off a sweet scent of fresh pine and juniper. A straggly skein of crows made black punctuation marks against the blue, the strident cawing cutting awkwardly through the sweeter song of the brush-dwelling birds.

He studied the cut in the clearer light of day.

As he had guessed, it was a perfect ambush point. The trail below wound up from a tree-bound meadow through more timber. Out from the meadow it got narrow and steep, flanked on both sides by high walls of soil too knotted with roots to chance riding across. It emerged on a tiny plateau, sheer-sided to the south, and banked with vertical rock walls to the north. The west side was a jumble of rough stone. Northwards the trail bled out between the walls of rock that ran steep and thin to a second plateau. There, the rock fanned out and round to form a shallow bowl like a natural amphitheatre. The cut opened like a knife slash on the northwest face. It went up at an angle to the main wall, wide enough at the entrance to take three horses riding abreast, but then it narrowed down over a three hundred yard length to a funnel that was only just wide enough to take a single rider. Like Billy Eagle had promised, there was no other way up.

Azul grinned without any humour showing on his face and moved back to the egress point. He hunkered down with his back against the bole of a stunted cedar and levered a shell into the breech of the Winchester. Below him, hidden amongst the trees, a bluejay screamed.

'They're coming,' he called softly. 'You ready?'

'Sure.' The *click!* of Billy Eagle's Winchester punctuated the statement as the hammer snapped back. 'I'm ready.'

Jimmy Witt came into the bowl. He was on foot, with his hat slung by the cord over his back. His red hair was plastered down with sweat, and his grubby white shirt had dark stains under the arms and down the chest. He held the sawed-off in front of his gut. There was a Colt tucked inside the strained band of his dark grey pants.

His little green eyes scanned the clearing from the shade of the trees. Then he waved his left hand above his head and five horsemen came out into the bowl. One was leading a riderless horse.

Azul didn't recognise any of them, except Witt.

They gathered around the red-head, who mopped his face with a bright red bandanna and said, 'They must've gone that way.' His voice carried clearly through the now-silent morning air. He pointed at the cut. A horse snorted nervously, lifting its tail to drop a steaming load of excrement onto the grass. A short, thin man with a straggly mustache said, 'Good place for an ambush, Jimmy.'

Witt shook his head, 'No better'n below, Mose. They wanted to hit us, they'd've done it by now. I reckon they're runnin'. Fast an' feared.'

'So you go in front.' Mose had a nasal, West Texas accent. 'You're so damn' certain.'

Jimmy Witt looked at the cut. Shrugged. Climbed astride his horse. He cocked the shotgun. Without speaking, he walked the pony over the grass and entered the cut. The others followed him.

For a few moments he was hidden from sight as the cut angled to the west. Then he came back into view as it curved round again and began to narrow out as it got steeper.

Azul lay flat on his belly with his right cheek tight against the sun-warmed stock of the Winchester. He watched Jimmy Witt move slowly up the path. He lined the blade of the foresight between the vee of the rearsight, angling the rifle down.

He squeezed the trigger.

Flame and a blurt of powder smoke erupted from the muzzle. Jimmy Witt's horse grunted and went down with a .44-40 calibre slug planted in its brain. The fat red-head went over the neck. He landed heavily, both hands stretched out in front to break his fall. They hit the hard stone of the cut and blood showed on his palms. More on his face, where his nose mashed against the rock. Azul traversed the rifle, swinging his sights on the last horse in the line. He killed it. Then shot the rider, a tall, sandy-haired man with a Mexican sombrero hiding his face.

Azul's bullet went in through his chest as he was lifting clear of his dying pony with a Spencer .41 carbine in his hands. The bullet plucked through his breastbone, deflecting slightly downwards so that it tore into a lung and lodged against a rib. The man screamed and began to spit blood. He went on spitting blood as Azul raked the cut with fire. His blue denim shirt got covered with it, the material staining dark as he knelt down with his head thrown back and a high, shrill scream erupting from his open mouth. After a while he keeled over and was still.

Billy Eagle was firing at random. His shots spanged off the stone walls, ricochetting back and forth so that the distorted lead was joined by chips of rock. Two men got blinded by the fragments of stone, lowering their guns as they rubbed at their eyes and tried to turn their mounts round. The horses squealed in panic as the gun thunder filled the cut and sharp, hot pieces of stone spattered against their flanks.

One man fell from the saddle and got trampled to death. He kept the reins in his left hand and a Colt's Army model in his right. He was firing blind, hurting his companions more than the two ambushers. And then his horse reared up and drove a hoof down against his chest. The man screamed. And shot the horse in the belly. It began to buck even more. A second hoof landed against his face and there was the soggy sound of flesh driving into bone. The cheek and jaw impacted as the man's face squashed. His left eye burst from the socket, hanging over his cheek as blood covered the orb. Then the hoofs came down again and the thin tendrils were severed as the eye was crushed and a thick spurt of brain matter flooded onto the ground.

Billy Eagle shot the other blinded man through the mouth. The mouth was wide open in a scream, so the bullet tore clear through his neck, opening a gaping hole that fountained a great spurt of blood over his back. He dropped his Winchester and pressed both hands to his throat, fighting to stem the blood. A ricochet hit the side of his head, and his temple smashed inwards. His eyes seemed to disappear into his skull, leaving only blood-filled sockets that stared sightlessly at the chaos as his body jerked and fell back.

Azul saw the fourth and fifth men trying to ride their ponies over Jimmy Witt's dead horse. One was unarmed, clutching at a shoulder massively damaged by Billy's ricochets. He shot the man in the belly, lifting him backwards off the pony with blood spraying vertically into the smoky air. The bullet ruptured the spleen and glanced off a rib, lodging under the shoulder so that the man twisted sideways as he fell and crashed onto his head. The other went down cleaner. He was – amazingly – unwounded. Azul shot him fast and tight through the left eye. The slug pulped the frightened blue sphere and emerged from the hindpart of the skull. It took a huge chunk of bone with it, spraying out in shards that danced on a spurting of crimson and sticky grey brain matter.

Azul turned, peering up the cut through the drifting clouds of smoke to where Jimmy Witt was clambering for the high ground. The fat red-head was using both hands to haul himself upwards, the shotgun dangling from its carrying strap. The back of his shirt was black now, with sweat, and his hat was lost.

Azul rose to his feet and began to run after him.

Jimmy Witt was cursing as he dragged himself up the slope. Cursing Azul and Billy Eagle and Cole Stanton. Cursing Art Durant and Joel Meek for not coming with him. Cursing himself for feeling too goddam confident.

Jimmy Witt was thirty years old. His parents owned — so far as he knew — a farm in Missouri. Jimmy had been sixteen years old when he quit the farm to join a friend called Jesse James to fight for the Southern cause under the command of a man called Quantrill. That was how he met Joel Meek, and through Meek, Cole Stanton.

Joel had been a trusted lieutenant of Quantrill's, and despite the giant's sexual tastes, he had become a friend of Jimmy's. When the Civil War ended they had ridden together for a while, robbing stage coaches and the odd train. Then Joel had met Art Durant, and Jimmy had drifted clear. He didn't like sharing a camp fire with two grunting, lusting men.

For a spell he had worked the Border country. Hiring out as bodyguard or shotgun rider, patrolling range : taking any work he could find.

And then he got word from Joel again. The big man had a place with an Eastern businessman called Stanton. Joel was in California then, but Stanton was moving out to Arizona and wanted reliable gunhands to protect his interests. Jimmy had understood the words not written in the letter and headed straight for Chandler's Butte. For a year he had lived high on the hog : Stanton paid well, and most of all of what Jimmy had to do, was scare people.

Until Billy Eagle showed up with his Spanish gold. And then the other goddam halfbreed. The one called Azul. Or just Breed, he'd heard.

And that one frightened him.

Jimmy Witt dragged his oversized beergut across the rim of the ridge and lay panting on the grass. He turned his head, looking down at the cleft. There was a whole lot of smoke down there, but no more gun fire. Horses were screaming, but there was no gun fire.

Maybe he had a chance.

He eased over the rim and rolled on his back. His breath was coming hard now, and his fingers trembled as they shunted fresh loads into the twin chambers of the cut-down Remington.

He got both barrels loaded and snapped the shotgun closed. He began to stand up.

And then a foot slammed against his face, smashing him back against the grass. He tried to lift the shotgun, but a second foot settled on the muzzles and pinned the gun against the ground. He reached for the Colt tucked into his belt. The ugly black hole of a Winchester's muzzle drove against his lips and a voice that was harsh and guttural said, 'Don't.'

Jimmy Witt squinted past the barrel of the Winchester and saw cold blue eyes looking at his face. The eyes held death. He decided that coffins shouldn't be draped with black : they should be draped with a very cold, icy blue.

He said : 'Oh, Jesus !'

Azul said, 'That's not my name.'

'Please,' said Jimmy Witt. 'Please.'

'Throw the gun away,' said Azul. 'Then talk.'

Jimmy took the Colt very carefully, very slowly, from his belt and tossed it away over the grass. Then he eased the carrying strap of the shotgun over his head and pushed the gun away.

Azul picked it up, backing clear of the terrified fat man. He lowered the hammer of the Winchester and tossed the rifle to one side.

'I told you I would kill you,' he said. 'But you didn't want what the others wanted, so I'll give you a chance.'

'They're faggots!' said Witt. 'Jesus Christ! I never wanted to go along with that. I never have.'

'You went along far enough,' said Azul. 'You held me while Joel Meek beat me.'

'I didn't have no choice,' moaned Jimmy. 'What else could I do?'

'You don't have a choice now,' said Azul; cold and deadly, 'Except what I give you.'

He backed away, covering twelve feet of ground in easy strides. He dropped the shotgun midway between them.

'If you can reach that,' he said. 'Reach it and kill me with it, you'll go free.'

Jimmy Witt wondered why he'd ever listened to Jesse. Or to Joel. Or to Stanton.

'You'll shoot me,' he said. 'You still got a gun.'

Azul lifted the Colt's Frontier from the holster and tossed it alongside the Winchester.

As his right hand was spread out, Jimmy Witt came up on his feet with more speed than any man that fat had a right to use. He threw himself at the Remington scattergun with his left hand scooped out to clutch the twin barrels and his right curling over the familiar grip to sink the forefinger over the trigger.

Azul went forwards at the same time.

His right hand flashed to his belt, fingers closing on the hilt of the Bowie knife. The heavy blade came clear of the sheath. Lifted up.

Drove down.

Jimmy Witt was turning the shotgun as the point of the knife drove through the apex of his skull. It went in through the top of his head, slicing his brain as Azul dropped to his knees, putting the full weight of his muscular body into the blow. Jimmy Witt's eyes started open. Like ferrets lurching out of their holes. His hands snatched clear of the shotgun as rictus action snapped his head back.

Azul twisted the knife.

Withdrew it.

And brought the blade down, double-gripped, against the hole.

Jimmy Witt's skull split apart like a severed melon. It split all the way to the bridge of his nose. His hair got redder as blood gouted from his cranium, and his eyes stared wildly to either side in reversal of a squint.

Inside the sundered skull the brain dripped fluids that were swiftly covered with crimson. His eyes paled over, becoming opaque. His belly trembled and he reared back on his knees with long streamers of bloody snot gusting from his face. A dark stain appeared over the front of his pants, matching the thicker spilling from the seat of his trousers. His fingers scrabbled madly against the grass, and then he pitched over, landing face-downwards. Thin streamers of pussy-looking grey erupted from his skull. His toes rammed a brief tattoo against the ground.

Azul stood back as flies began to settle on the feast. High above, a crow called.

The halfbreed looked up. The crows he had seen earlier were coming back, swooping low over the trees. Above them were the larger shapes of buzzards and vultures, descending on a slow spiral.

He drove his knife deep into the ground. Tugged it free, and wiped it on the grass. He looked at Jimmy Witt's sundered head, then turned as Billy Eagle came out onto the meadow.

'Jesus Christ!' Billy stopped, gaping at the corpse. 'What you do to him?'

'He was stupid,' rasped Azul. 'He should have known better than to come up a trail like that.'

'That's one of Stanton's men,' said Billy. 'Jimmy Witt.'

'He was still stupid,' said Azul. 'Now he's a half-Witt.'

CHAPTER EIGHT

They rode away through a brightening day, climbing higher into the Piñon Llanos as the sun climbed over the sky and the circle of black birds closed down on the cut.

'Funny that Cobly wasn't with them,' said Billy. 'Him being the peace officer an' us being jailbreakers.'

'Not really,' murmured Azul. 'He's more use to Stanton in Chandler's Butte.'

'How's that?' asked the halfbreed Mimbreño. 'How you figger that?'

'Stanton wants your gold,' said Azul, slowly; thinking it out. 'He can claim a murder charge against you now. Back it with the new killings. When the circuit judge arrives, he can swear out a deposition. With Cobly to back him, the judge could assign the gold to Stanton.'

'So it'd be legal?' asked Billy. 'To take it off of me?'

'I think,' said Azul. 'Something like that.'

'So what do we do?' Billy looked worried. 'What now?'

'*We?*' Azul shrugged. 'I thought you didn't want to show me the mine.'

'*Madre de Dios!*' grunted Billy. 'That was before. I think that right now we'd better get there as fast as we can. I guess I trust you now.'

'*Enjuh!*' said Azul. 'Let's go.'

'*Si*,' Billy answered. 'You're right.'

They took off at a fast canter, riding through a perfect day. The sun was up high, hot enough to lift sweat from the horses and men alike. Shining clear from a sky now devoid of cloud : a great, brilliant spread of azure that was almost hurtful to look at.

They continued until noon. Halted to eat. Then rode on.

Four days later they reached Billy Eagle's camp.

Billy led the way into the meadow. Azul stripped the saddle from the grey stallion and left it cropping grass alongside the bay gelding. Billy guided him up the steep path to the ledge.

'Jesus ! Whiskey.' Billy went inside the cave to find a bottle.

Azul dropped his saddle outside, waiting.

It was around noon. The sun was high, slanting vertical shadows down the rock face. Azul drank water from his canteen, shaking his head when Billy offered him the bottle.

'I'll show you the mine,' said Billy. 'You come this far, you may as well see it.'

Azul nodded and stood up.

They went down a wide ledge to what looked like a sheer drop. For twenty, maybe thirty, feet there was nothing but space. The ledge ended at a shallow wall of dropped shale. It looked precariously balanced, slid down from higher up to gather between the rims of the ledge. Below, it faded down over a near-vertical face. Upwards of the wall, there was nothing but bare stone, rising to a vee-shape that was overhung with gristly trees and gnarled roots.

. Billy Eagle lifted a bush aside and pointed at a knotted rope that was fastened to the trees in a succession of hidden descents. Or ascents.

Azul began to climb.

He came out onto a game trail. Narrow as a mustang's ribs. Bordered on both sides, up and down, by trees. He waited until Billy Eagle joined him.

The halfbreed pointed up the slope.

'We go that way.'

Azul climbed again.

Twenty feet up Billy Eagle joined him once more and led the way across a precipitous drop that was lined with only the extended roots of the big oaks and the cedars. The face was sheer, the only footholds the roots. Beneath them there was nothing but the gap that fell down into the split.

They came out on the far side and descended an equally sheer slope to what was left of the game trail.

Billy Eagle reached under a massive root that spread, thick as a growing pine, for a rope. He tossed it down the face of the cliff and said, 'There's steps. They been worn out, but you can use them still.'

Azul took hold of the rope and eased clear of the ledge. He saw his footholds, just like Billy had told him. They were very steep and very narrow. And most had been eroded, so that all they did was afford a precarious footing for the descent to the cave below.

He swung inside the entrance and shook the rope to let Billy know it was now free.

He waited until the Mimbreño halfbreed joined him.

Billy picked up a torch and a match. He struck the match against the wall of the cave and lit the torch. Light shone on cold, grey stone. Azul followed him inside.

There was a smell of must. Like old men's socks. Or opened tombs. Two skeletons were spread either side of the wider part of the interior cave. A rotting dagger dangled from the ribs of one, the other was crouched over a rusting pistol.

Azul ignored them, staring at the wealth stacked inside the cave. High as a man's waist, and equally spread across, there were gold bars. The pile was around four feet high. Four wide on each side. The floor of the cave was littered with gems that glistened in the torch light.

'I think you found Eldorado,' murmured Azul. 'Or something like that.'

'Eldorado?' asked Billy. 'What's that?'

'A legend,' answered Azul. 'It don't exist. Until now.'

'What you think it's worth?' asked Billy. 'You know more about it than me.'

Azul looked at the gold. Looked down at the floor. He bent to scoop up a handful of stones.

'Millions,' he said. 'You could be the richest man in the world.'

'*Santissimo!*' Billy waved the torch around his head, sending streamers of light through the cave. 'Let's go have a drink on that!'

Azul stood up, dropping the diamonds he was holding back into the dust of the cave's floor.

'Sure,' he said. 'Let's have a drink.'

Back inside Billy's cave it was warm and friendly. There was a fire built up far enough inside that the glow wouldn't show outside the entrance. Deer meat roasted on the spit and a pot of coffee bubbled over the flames. Billy was drinking whiskey.

'So I'm rich?' he asked. 'Really rich?'

Azul nodded and reached out to tear a hunk of meat from the roast.

'Rich as anyone,' he said. 'Richer than most.'

'Jesus!' said Billy. 'I'll buy Chandler's Butte. I'll buy all the best whiskey an' all the best girls. I'll buy anything I want.'

'If you can,' said Azul. 'If Stanton lets you.'

'I'm rich,' said Billy. 'I can do what I want.'

'You think so?' asked Azul. 'You really think so?'

'Why not?' said Billy. 'Why shouldn't I?'

'You're a halfbreed,' said Azul. 'You know what that means?'

'Means I know what it's like to get spat on,' grunted Billy. 'Hear folks whisperin' *squawman* behind my back. No more, though. Ain't no one gonna talk like that no more. Not to Billy Eagle.'

He stretched on his blanket, shoulders propped against the red-lit stone of the cave. He lifted the bottle to his mouth. Emptied it and tossed aside. There was the harsh sound of glass striking empty glass. He uncorked a fresh bottle and took a deep swallow. His dark eyes were bright.

'I'll get me a house,' he said slowly. 'A real house. I'll buy some land. Maybe raise cows. Or horses. I'll take me a trip to St. Louis an' buy me some girls. I'll buy me a girl for every day of the week, an' if I get bored with 'em, I'll pay 'em off and buy some more. I'll get me some fancy clothes an' a buggy with a matched team. No one'll spit on me then. No one'll say *squawman*.'

'Not to your face,' murmured Azul, remembering something old See-Both-Ways had once told him.

He had been about nineteen then, and had just returned to the *rancheria* after trading off a string of mustangs. He had sold the ponies in a place called Sutter's Crossing, on the Gila. Two American buyers had been looking for cattle stock, and when the young halfbreed stated his price, they had laughed.

Azul had accepted that : he had never expected to get that high a price for unbroken animals : it was all part of the horse trading. But gradually the laughter had turned sour. Insults had crept into the dealing. *Red nigger. Squawman's leavings. Goddam 'breed.* A fight had begun, leaving Azul with a bloody nose and cut eye. One *pinda-lick oyi* was left with a broken arm, the other with two broken ribs and a face that resembled a pulped tomato. Azul had taken his money and left the horses.

Why? he had asked the Chiricahua shaman. *Why should they hate me?*

Because you are *a halfbreed,* the old man had replied. *I think that frightens them. They cannot know just how to handle you. If they were dealing with a whiteman, then they would look on him as an equal. If they were dealing with a full-blood Indian, then they would look down on him. You stand between: they don't know what you are.*

What does a dog do when it meets something strange? Something it doesn't know?

Barks, Azul had replied. *Perhaps attacks.*

Why?

Because it gets frightened, the young man had replied. *Because it attacks what it doesn't know.*

You see? Sees-Both-Ways had said. *You answer your own question.*

There had been a pause then, and the old man had stared into the glowing embers of his fire. Then he spoke again :

A whiteman. Some whitemen, anyway, think they have the right to take what they want from the Indians. They think we are like a tree they can hack down to clear a place for them to live in. Like a stone they kick from their path. A halfbreed is different: he has white blood in his veins and is not quite Indian, so he is harder to handle. They see their own blood mingled with the red, and — like the dog — are frightened.

I don't see why, Azul had said.

If you could see that, Sees-Both-Ways had answered, *then you would be wiser than I.*

'It won't be that easy,' he said to Billy Eagle. 'It'll be hard.'

'Why?' asked the man. 'I got the money.'

'You got to keep it,' replied Azul. 'That's the hard part.'

'Chandler's Butte ain't the only place with an assay office,' said Billy. 'I can go to Jameston. Ballard, even. Stanton don't own them.'

'Maybe not,' murmured Azul. 'But he's got the money to hire men, and he's got the greed. Now he's got a score to settle, too. He'll keep on looking.'

'He won't find this place.' Billy sucked more whiskey. 'No one's ever found this place except me.'

Azul shrugged. 'Maybe Stanton wasn't that desperate until now. Hell! You was taking the gold to him and selling it cheap. Now he knows the supply's dried up and he's lost six men.'

'So what you think he'll do?' asked Billy.

'Put all his muscle into finding us,' said Azul slowly. 'Try real hard to locate us.'

'So what do we do?' The grin left Billy's face.

'What the hell do we do?'

'They say halfbreeds are second best,' Azul murmured. 'So we'll try harder.'

CHAPTER NINE

Vance Cobly lived in a single-storey frame house with a neat, white picket out in front. There were flowers growing in his garden, and a stunted apple tree that was fighting to survive. The porch was freshly painted and the lace curtains behind the panes of the front window were spotlessly clean.

Cole Stanton tapped on the screen door. He was dressed up for visiting in a dove-grey suit and shiny boots. He wore grey gloves on his hands and carried a silver-topped walking cane. He doffed a dove-grey hat with a black silk band as the door opened, and smiled at the woman.

She was small and plump. She looked as if she could get fat if she stopped worrying. Her hair was a rich brown, tinted with streaks of grey. It was pulled back in a bun from a face that was still pretty, despite the frown lines. She wore a blue gingham dress with a big white apron covering her ample bosom. There was a smudge of flour on her cheek.

'Elizabeth?' Stanton ducked his head. 'How are you?'

'Well, thank you.' Her voice was soft, accented with the remnant of a brogue. 'What do you want?'

'How's Vance?'

'Hungry,' said the sheriff's wife. 'He can't eat nothing but soup.'

'That bad?' Stanton fidgetted with his cane. 'May I see him?'

Elizabeth Cobly stepped aside to let the pale-faced man into the house. She closed the door and bustled to the rear, calling over her shoulder: 'You know where to find him.'

Stanton went into a tiny parlour. There was a circular rug at the centre of the polished floor. A small table at the centre of the rug, with a chipped vase holding some yellow prairie roses. A big, dark-wood dresser with a glass front covered one wall. Facing the dresser on the other wall was a daguerrotype in a shiny mahogany frame. It showed Vance Cobly, hatless in a dark suit, with one arm around Elizabeth, in a white bridal gown. The room was warm and stuffy. Vance Cobly was slumped in a wing-sided chair with the plush wearing bare behind his head. He had a white bandage wrapped under his jaw, fastened on top of his head. More bandage covered one side of his face.

Stanton pulled off his gloves and set them neatly on the table. Set the cane alongside. He reached under his frock-coat and set a flat bottle beside the gloves.

'Thought you might use a drink, Vance.'

Cobly said something that sounded like 'Thanks.' It was hard to tell.

Stanton uncorked the bottle and passed it to the lawman. He carried a high-backed, cane-bottomed chair over to face Cobly. Sat down.

'Doc said the 'breed smashed it in three places.' His voice was dry and whispery. Like a spider's legs scuttling over dust. 'It hurt?'

Cobly nodded.

'They killed Jimmy Witt,' said Stanton. 'Him and five others. Massacred them. There's a service to-morrow.'

'You found them?' The way Cobly's jaw was smashed it came out like, '*Uffindem?*'

Stanton shook his head. 'Not yet. But we will. I sent Art Durant and Joel Meek over to Jameston, and more men to Ballard. Way I see it, they won't chance coming back here, so Billy's got to find some other place to cash the gold. Jameston and Ballard are the only towns inside a two month ride he can do that. I also got men scouring the Piñons. They find them murdering halfbreeds, they'll bring them back here to get hung.'

'Judge,' mumbled Cobly. 'When's he due?'

'Got word yesterday,' said Stanton. 'That's why I'm here. He should arrive in about three weeks time. It's not Judge Yardlom. He got shot by some Mexican he was sending to the pen. There's a new man. A fellow called Cantwell. Abel Cantwell. That's the problem : he's got a reputation for sympathising with the Indians. We might just need to do some hard talking to persuade him that gold belongs to us.'

'We?' asked Cobly. 'Us?'

It sounded like *Ooee* and *Ugh*.

'Hell, yes.' Stanton looked round for a glass. Found none, so took a shot from the bottle. He coughed and wiped his mouth on a pale, grey silk kerchief. 'I want this whole thing legal. No questions asked afterwards. If you back me, then we can get those two halfbreeds on a murder charge. Get that find signed over all legal, and split the profits. Just like I promised.'

'All right.' Cobly forced the words to come out more or less clear. 'I'll back you.'

'Good,' said Stanton. 'Fine. There's just one more thing. Art and Joel are both wearing deputies badges. You'll need to say you swore them in;

fill out the papers. In case.'

Cobly nodded and lifted the bottle again. His eyes looked tired and he winced as the liquor hit his gums.

Stanton stood up, reaching for his gloves. 'Fine, Vance. That's very good. Just remember how much money you got coming, and say the right thing.'

'Yes,' said Cobly, making it sound like *Eth*.

Stanton pulled on the gloves and lifted his cane. 'I'll keep you in touch, Vance. Take it easy.'

Cobly nodded and took another long pull on the bottle.

Stanton smiled and went out through the door. He closed it carefully behind him. Set his hat on his head. Then turned as the kitchen door opened. Elizabeth Cobly came out.

'Vance hasn't told me what's going on,' she said quietly, 'but I guess it's something to do with that gold Billy Eagle found. I don't care about that. I do care about Vance. Don't you hurt him, Cole. You hurt him, I'll get to you. I promise.'

'Elizabeth.' Stanton touched the brim of his hat. 'I wouldn't hurt either of you.'

The woman went on looking at him as she opened the door. Her hand left a smear of flour on the polished brass. After it closed behind Stanton's lean figure she rubbed at it for a long time. Like someone trying to wipe away a bad memory.

Azul sat the grey stallion inside the shadow of a wide-limbed oak. It grew out over the edge of a short ridge that banked onto a wide, flat stand of grass. Beyond the grass the ridge got steeper and deeper, falling away a hundred feet or more to a stream that ran out from a hole in the ground and

98

cut over the flatlands below to disappear again amongst the trees. A group of around fifteen riders was coming up the water. They were spread out in a line, staggered into separate bunches. They were all studying the ground.

The halfbreed watched them as they reached the source of the water. Watched them bunch up and then circle out to the confines of the grass. Then turn back and begin to cut up the slope.

He ducked his head under the branches and walked the stallion slowly out from under the tree. Then he turned the horse eastwards to where the original source of the stream entered the ridge and splashed into the pebble-covered bottom. He rode the grey horse along the course of the water until he came to a wide shelf of naked rock. He urged the pony out and crossed the rock, leaving it where a narrow deer trail came down from the timber. He followed the game trail for about a mile, then turned north along a flank of land thick with loam and the high, shady bulks of oak and cypress. After a while the flank gave onto a higher ridge. Azul topped it and halted.

From the fresh vantage point he was looking down into a wide, elongated valley. The sides were too steep to hold much timber, and the bottom was mostly sand with only a sparse clustering of grass showing through. There was a second group of five men moving cautiously along the base of the valley.

Azul turned the stallion around and rode to the head. He crossed over into the next valley and skirted round a shale slope to crest the facing ridge and go in amongst the trees again.

Where the valley lifted up to the downspill of the

mountains there was a plateau. It was bare of timber or grass, a high, wide spread of bare stones that glistened in the sun, the dark, blue-grey rock shining bright, almost golden, under the brilliance.

Nine men were combing over the stone. They were bunched together, and like all the other groups, they rode with rifles and carbines in their hands.

Azul pulled the reins over, taking the grey pony's head down the slope. He dug his heels against the flanks and went down at a breath-taking run that brought him out onto a meadow. He crossed the grass and swung over into a stand of timber, slowing as he reached the trees. He rode through them for two miles, then urged the grey onto a shale slide and leant back in the saddle as the big horse slithered, butt-down, to the bottom. After that, he cut into another stream. Followed it along to where it opened into a pool, and swam the horse across to the rocky bank. Up from the pool there was a steep slope of hard-packed sand. Azul went up it, cresting the ridge beyond to come out into a series of folds that were dense with trees. He rode fast through them and then followed a ridge along to Billy Eagle's camp.

The Mimbreño halfbreed was sitting inside his cave with a bottle of whiskey beside him and a small stack of gold bars in front.

'They're looking hard,' said Azul. 'Not close yet, but looking.'

'They won't find us,' said Billy. 'Have a drink.'

Azul shook his head.

'I saw three groups,' he said. 'Close on thirty men. That's enough to find us. Just by chance.'

'So what we do?' Billy lifted the bottle. 'What can we do?'

'Get some help,' said Azul. 'Find us some friends.'

'Friends?' gaped Billy Eagle. 'I didn't know us halfbreeds had any.'

'They're where you find them,' murmured Azul. 'Right now, I'm going looking.'

CHAPTER TEN

The column of smoke rose like an exclamation mark into the windless sky. Azul dropped a bundle of green branches onto the fire and lifted his blanket. When the smoke was turned a thick black, he spread the blanket over the source. Lifted it clear. Spread it again. The column of smoke broke up into a series of individual clouds that drifted heavenwards at seemingly random intervals. After a while, Azul dropped the blanket and scanned the surrounding hills.

He was on a high ridge, not far from the topmost summit of the Piñon Llanos, miles from Billy Eagle's camp. He waited, watching the unbroken column of smoke drift upwards. Time passed and he began to move the blanket again, repeating his motions so that a fresh series of signals rose towards the sky.

This time they were answered by a drift of smoke from a slightly lower ridge some five miles distant. Azul watched the smoke, then stamped his fire dead. He stowed the blanket back on the grey stallion and climbed into the saddle. He went down the ridge and began to climb the facing slope. When he reached the crest, he was in a long, wide clearing. Trees flanked the grass on all sides. There was a dead fire at the centre. Azul dismounted, ground-hitching his horse. He left his Winchester in the boot, and draped his gunbelt over the saddlehorn. Then he walked away from the pony and stood waiting.

A man came out from amongst the trees. He was

slightly shorter than Azul, but heavier muscled, with a wide, deep chest and bowed legs. His hair was long, straight and black, held off his broad face by a red bandanna. A dark blue vest hung open over his torso, and a loincloth hung from his waist. His naked legs were tucked into knee-high moccasins. He wore a wide leather belt with a sheathed knife on the left. He carried an old single-shot Spencer rifle. As he came closer, Azul saw that his face was very dark, with high cheekbones and a broad, flattish nose. His eyes were sunk deep enough that it was difficult to gauge his expression. His mouth was wide and straight, heavy of underlip.

He halted ten feet from Azul and said, 'Why do you ask the Chiricahua for help?'

'The Chiricahua are my brothers.' Azul stared at the man's face, ignoring the rifle pointed at his belly. 'I ask their help in the name of brotherhood.'

'You are the one they call Lobo.' The Apache used the Mexican slang for halfbreed. 'I have heard of you.'

'In the *rancheria* where I was born, my people called me Azul.' He said it casually, knowing that the Indian's acceptance of him was vital to his plan. 'My mother was Rainbow Hair of the Bedonkohe, from the line of Mangas Colorado.'

The Apache nodded, not moving his rifle. '*Enjuh!* But your father gave you a *pinda-lick-oyi* name, like his own.'

'My father helped the Chiricahua.' Azul was conscious of movement behind him. He resisted the temptation to turn. 'I would help them, too. In return for their help.'

The Apache nodded. 'I am Chikisin. How would you help me?'

Azul said: 'There is another lobo. A Mimbreño halfbreed called Billy Eagle. He has found some gold. Not a mine, but one of the places where the old Spanish hid their gold. There are whitemen trying to take it away from him.'

'We have seen the whitemen,' said Chikisin. 'And we know of Billy Eagle. We let him hunt deer.'

'The hunting has changed now,' replied Azul. 'The *pinda-lick-oyi* want to take the gold away and kill Billy Eagle. I have vowed to kill some of them. They beat me, and I would take my due. I ask you to guard the gold. To stop them taking it.'

'We must talk about this,' said Chikisin. 'This is a thing for all to decide.'

Azul nodded, and the muscular Apache lowered the rifle, waving his men in closer.

There were nine of them. Broncos, to judge from their unkempt appearance and hard eyes. They sat down in a circle with Azul and Chikisin facing one another. Azul noticed that none carried weapons more modern than the cap and ball Colts of the Civil War.

'Tell us why we should help you,' said Chikisin. 'If we kill whitemen up here, they will send the blue-coats to drive us out, and it is hard to fight the blue-coats with these old guns.'

'The gold could buy you new guns,' said Azul. 'The fast-firing guns the whitemen use. Better even than the guns the blue-coats carry.'

'That is true.' Chikisin smiled, a glint of humour showing in his deep-sunk eyes. 'So why should we not take the gold for ourselves?'

Azul smiled back. 'What would you do with it? Ride into a town and ask for guns? The *pinda-lick-oyi* would shoot you down.'

'We could trade,' argued Chikisin. 'We could go to Mexico.'

'You carry trade guns now.' Azul gestured contemptuously at the ancient weapons. 'That is what the traders will sell you, here or in Mexico. Even if you could get the fast-firing guns, they would take more gold than the guns are worth. And how would you get ammunition?'

'He speaks the truth.' The voice was soft, coming from the man on Chikisin's right. 'The traders sell us what the whitemen no longer use or want. And we cannot get ammunition.'

Azul glanced at the man. He was thin of face for an Apache, dressed in a faded blue cotton shirt. The grip of his Henry single-shot was bound with copper wire. He smiled at Azul.

The warrior on Chikisin's left was older and uglier. His nose was unnaturally flat where it had been broken. There was a long scar running across his cheek from the point of the break. He was naked from the waist up, his legs encased in loose-fitting white pants that were held up by a gunbelt. The holster was old and worn, the butt of a Colt's Navy model protruding from the leather. On his right side there were pouches containing the powder, balls and percussion caps. The pouches looked near empty.

He scowled and said, 'Why should we trust this lobo? Look at him. He wears the clothes of the *pinda-lick-oyi*. He carries the guns he talks about. I think he is more white than Apache. I think he wants to lure us into a trap.'

Azul loked hard at the warrier, his face coldly impassive. He lifted his right hand to the brim of his hat and swept the Sonoran stetson from his head. Dropped it on the grass. Then he reached inside his

shirt, drawing out the thin leather band the Chiricahua wore when fighting. He shook his mane of
sun-bleached hair back over his shoulders and tied
the war band in place around his forehead.

'I have made a vow,' he said. 'There were five men
had me beaten so that I would tell them where this
gold is. I vowed to kill them. One is already dead. To
kill the others, I need your help.'

The scar-faced Apache grunted, making a dismis-
sive gesture.

Chikisin looked at Azul.

'Naize says we should trust you. Cicatriz says not.
We must decide.'

He looked slowly round the circle of warriors.
Three men nodded; four shook their heads. Chikisin
shrugged.

'It is hard, Azul. Three and Naize is four. Four
and Cicatriz is five.' He lifted fingers as he spoke,
staring at his hands. 'I have heard stories of you told
in the *rancherias,* and I think I believe you, but if I
say *yes,* then it is five and five. That is not good for
a band such as this one. Not with the *pinda-lick-oyi*
coming into the mountains.'

'There is an easy way to decide it.' Cicatriz turned
his scarred face on Chikisin. 'If he is speaking the
truth, then he will fight for it. Let him fight me. If
he wins, I will do what he asks. If he loses . . .' He
smiled for the first time, staring at Azul like an undertaker measuring up a corpse.

Chikisin stared at Cicatriz. At Azul. At the
ground. Then he nodded. 'Very well. That is how it
will be.'

Azul was naked, save for his buckskin pants. Cicatriz faced him clad only in the faded cotton leggings.

The other Chiricahua stood round in a wide circle, watching; anticipating.

Cicatriz came forwards in a scuttling, sideways movement that was intended to shift Azul off balance. The blond-haired man – accustomed to Apache wrestling – moved inside the attack, knowing that Cicatriz was sounding him out. Watching in turn for some weakness in the older man.

Cicatriz moved round in a circle, arms thrust out to splay fingers at Azul's face. The halfbreed watched him, his own hands loose in front of his muscular body, waiting. Cicatriz began to chant insults. Then darted in with both arms lifted high. Azul took them, fingers interlocking. The two men stood for a moment like a human bridge; knuckles whitening as each tried to force the other's hands down. Then Cicatriz heaved back, still clutching Azul's hands as he raised one foot in a high kick.

Azul followed the movement, turning to the side so that the foot slid past his hip and he was coming round behind Cicatriz with the older man's arms dragged back to cross over Cicatriz's throat. Cicatriz let his fingers go limp. Slipped them clear of Azul's grasp and took hold of the wrists as he reversed his backwards roll and hauled Azul forwards over his head.

Azul felt himself lifted over the warrior's heavy shoulders. He curled just after the apex of the throw and brought his feet down in time to take the weight. He rolled back. Cicatriz was still clutching his wrists, taken by surprise at the sudden shift in balance. Azul thrust both legs out hard in front. His bare feet slammed into the Chiricahua's stomach and Cicatriz flew backwards.

Naize whooped encouragement.

Azul came up on his feet in the same rolling movement. He faced Cicatriz, circling again.

They closed. Cicatriz ducked under Azul's arms and fastened a lock on the right leg. Azul was thrown off balance. He felt his leg doubled under him and turned on his out-thrust hands, swiping his free leg against the Chiricahua's ankles. Cicatriz went down. Azul jerked clear. Rolled, and came up on his feet while the other man was still on his knees. He aimed a kick at the man's stomach, but Cicatriz caught it, twisting the foot so that Azul fell down again, on his face. The Apache landed on his back in a cat-like spring. Arms heavy with sinew looped under Azul's, the hands cupping behind his neck. Cicatriz began to bend Azul forwards, lifting his elbows so that the halfbreed's arms were raised up, counterpointed tension mounting in his spine. Azul got to his knees. His chin was forced down against his chest and it was getting hard to breath. He slumped into the pressure, then rammed backward, forcing Cicatriz under him. The grip broke.

Azul writhed to the side and lifted his right arm. He brought it down, palm open, against the Chiricahua's face. Cicatriz's head slammed against the ground. Azul twisted, lifting again onto his knees, this time with his hands clasped and his elbows pointed downwards. They slammed against the Chiricahua's belly. Cicatriz grunted, his head lifting as his body doubled over. Azul punched him in the mouth. Hard. Hard enough that his knuckles were cut on the teeth as they mashed the warrior's lips back.

Cicatriz twisted on one hand and landed a kick on Azul's left knee. He reached out to clutch the second descending fist and tugged Azul off balance again.

Teeth snapped close by the halfbreed's left ear, and he jerked his head away. The Chiricahua's legs closed on his waist, scissoring about his midriff as Cicatriz reached up to fasten powerful fingers over his face. Azul closed his eyes to avoid the probing nails and bit down on the fingers in his mouth. He ground his teeth together and the grip went away. He reached down to grasp the entwined moccasins and turned the feet apart. Cicatriz's hands found his throat and began to squeeze. Azul shoved back again, slamming his elbows against the warrior's ribs. Cicatriz laughed and went on squeezing.

Lights began to flash across Azul's eyes. There was a raw pounding inside his skull and a terrible pain in his chest. He reached up, sinking his fingers over the clutching wrists so that the tips dug against the insides. He began to squeeze. The grip on his throat loosened and he forced it aside.

Both men came to their feet. Cicatriz was shedding blood from his mouth and nose. Azul was gasping for breath, his face pale.

They closed again.

Azul turned Cicatriz with a hip throw, then got slung over the Apache's head when he tried to end the fight. Cicatriz got an arm lock on the halfbreed and lost it when Azul smashed his legs from under him. Both men were sweating heavily.

Then Cicatriz tried to end it with a desperate move. He came in at a run, arms out to circle Azul's waist. The halfbreed waited until the arms were almost in position, then brought his knee up against the Chiricahua's chin as his clenched fists landed against the back of the man's neck. Cicatriz's mouth snapped closed. His head snapped back. His eyes opened wide. Closed, fast. Then opened again and swung slowly shut.

Azul staggered back.

'Well?' He looked at the surrounding Apaches. 'Will you help me now?'

Cicatriz opened his eyes. They were hazed. 'You do not fight like an Apache,' he said.

'I learned from the whitemen,' answered the half-breed. 'Sometimes that way can be better.'

'It taught you how to beat me,' acknowledged the Chiricahua. 'Maybe you are right.'

'It is settled.' Chikisin's voice was firm. 'We ride with Azul.'

'You're crazy,' grumbled Billy Eagle. 'They'll steal me blind.'

'No.' Azul shook his head. 'Chikisin gave me his word.'

'But I'll hafta to give them my gold,' moaned the halfbreed. '*Jesus Cristo!* I worked long enough for that.'

'Only a little,' said Azul. 'Enough to buy guns so they can defend you. You don't give it to them, Stanton will take the lot.'

'They can't buy guns,' argued Billy. 'Gold's no use to them.'

'We can,' said Azul. 'In Jameston. When we take the next load in.'

'What?' Billy lifted his bottle. 'That's crazy. We'll get arrested again.'

'No.' Azul sipped coffee. 'It's not crazy; it's the only way. We take some of the gold to Jameston and use some of the cash to buy guns and ammunition. Then you got a regular guard that Stanton can't pass.'

'So we ride down to Jameston,' said Billy, 'an' trade a few gold bars for rifles and ammunition. An' no one asks us a question about what we're doin', or where we're takin' the guns? That's crazy.'

'No,' Azul repeated. 'I got it worked out.'

'You better have,' mumbled Billy. 'You better have it worked out real good.'

'We leave tomorrow,' said Azul. 'At dawn.'

He left Billy Eagle with his bottles and went down to the meadow where the ten bronco Chiricahua were waiting. He explained his plan to them and they accepted it, fading out into the surrounding timber like slinking cougars anticipating a rich kill.

The dawn brought a threat of rain. The sun shone from under an overlay of dark stormclouds, its rays glancing off the underside of the black-bellied clouds like sparks from an anvil. The air was moist, the birdsong muted. There was a stillness over the mountains.

Azul drank coffee. Billy Eagle drank coffee laced with whiskey. They both ate fried deermeat.

Then they mounted up and rode away to the north.

Billy Eagle led the way down to the Mamacita and cut off in the direction of the Gila. The country on that side of the Piñon Llanos range was empty of Stanton's hunters, and they made good time up to where the Gila branched with the Llañita stream.

It was a three week ride before they got to Jameston. And then Azul insisted they wait until nightfall before going in.

Jameston was fractionally larger than Chandler's Butte. It spread down a valley of the Gila like a scab on the face of the hills. Once it had been a mining town, and the memories lingered on in the empty pocking of the diggings surrounding the town. The old mine workings stared at the newer houses like the empty eye sockets of bleached skulls. Rusting rails bled down the valley sides like the dried-up pourings of a giant's body. Many of the houses were empty, the remaining buildings frantic with the attempt to maintain a semblance of life that was dying out from under them.

There was a wide street that spanned a quarter mile of the valley. At both ends there were deserted houses. At the centre there was a saloon and a dry goods store; a milliners and an eatery; a stage office and a stable; a hardware store and a hotel. There was also a sheriff's office with a small jail attached at the back.

Azul headed for that.

He rode in amongst the dilapidated houses surrounding mainstreet. Found an alley that was flanked by empty buildings and tethered his horse. Billy Eagle came with him as he paced up to the jail.

There was a light burning out front. Underneath it there was a short, thin man smoking a cigar with his bootheels up on the porch rail and a badge sharding light off his chest.

Azul came up on the sidewalk without the man hearing him. He pressed his Colt against the greying temple and said, 'Sheriff? Where's the assay office?'

The man didn't move, other than to stop his rocking.

'Why you want it?'

'Got a deposit to make.' Azul snaked a bar from under his shirt and dropped it over the lawman's crotch. 'Want to do it quietly.'

'Jesus!' The cigar dropped from the peace officer's mouth. Burned against his pants, unnoticed. 'You're the one they told me about.'

'Who told you?' Azul bent over to knock the smouldering cigar from the man's pants.

'Two fellers.' The lawman remained still under the pressure of the Colt. 'A big feller. Bearded. An' a fancy-pants. Said they was deputies from Chandler's Butte.'

'Names?' asked the halfbreed.

'Meek,' said the lawman. 'Joel Meek an' Art Durant. They said you might come here.'

'So now I've arrived,' said Azul. 'And I want to trade gold for cash.'

'Need the assay office fer that,' said the peace officer. 'It's closed.'

'We'll open it,' said Azul. 'Right now.'

The sheriff nodded. 'All right. Whatever you say.'

He stood up under Azul's prompting and led the way down the quiet street. Billy Eagle followed behind with a Winchester in his right hand and his left holding a bag filled with gold bars.

Azul kept the Colt shoved tight against the peace officer's spine as they cut clear of mainstreet into the alleys beyond. Two blocks up they came to a frame house with a dirty wire fence in front. The sheriff went up to the door and knocked.

A woman's voice said, 'Go away.'

'It's Lomax,' said the sheriff. 'It's important.'

'Why?' asked a man's voice. 'What is it?'

Lomax went on tapping on the door. After a while it opened and a man in a nightshirt, with tousled hair, stuck his head out and said, 'What the hell you want?'

Billy Eagle jammed his Winchester against Lomax's spine as Azul stepped past the lawman and thrust the muzzle of his Colt against the man's face.

'Oh, Jesus!' The door swung open as the man staggered back. 'I got no money here.'

Azul stepped inside the house, motioning for Billy to follow him. The Mimbreño halfbreed shoved Lomax inside and swung the door closed.

Azul said, 'We just want some gold assayed. And paid for.'

The woman's voice sounded again : 'Who the hell is it, Tom?'

'No one, sweetheart.' The assay clerk stared at the gun thrust into his belly. 'Just a little late business.'

'Jesus!' There was the sound of mattress springs creaking as a body turned. Then snores.

'They on the level?' The clerk directed his question at Lomax.

The peace officer shrugged. 'I'm alive. So far.'

'Get the keys,' said Azul. 'Fast.'

The assay office was part of the bank. Tom had keys for both. They went in through the back.

When Tom tested and weighed the five bars Billy Eagle had brought with him he whistled. 'Christ Jesus! These are worth close on five hundred apiece. That's near on two thousand five hundred dollars.'

'We'll take two thousand,' said Azul. 'The rest is yours. For keeping your mouths shut.'

Lomax and Tom nodded together like matched puppets.

Tom opened the safe and fetched out the bills. He counted them carefully into three piles. One for Azul and Billy Eagle, the other two for him and Lomax.

'Now I want rifles,' said Azul. 'Ten Winchesters, plus ammunition.'

'Nathan's over to the saloon,' said Tom.

'Why you want them?' said Lomax. 'You starting a war?'

'Something like that,' Azul replied. 'You want to

fetch him? Or do I take back your money?'

Lomax looked at the pile of bills. Looked at Tom. Tom shook his head and picked up his own pile. Lomax pursed his lips, then reached out to lift the money.

'All right,' he said. 'I'll fetch him.'

Azul grinned and lifted the Colt to touch Tom's face. 'No tricks, or your friend gets shot, and you get busted for taking bribes.'

Lomax nodded without speaking.

'Don't try anything,' said Azul. 'Unless you want to get killed.'

Lomax shook his head and made for the rear door. 'I'll bring him back here.'

'Good,' said Azul.

Around fifteen long minutes later Lomax reappeared with a tall, thin man dressed in a dun brown suit with a heavy gold watch chain strung across his vest.

'Nathan Fellows,' he said.

'They'll cost you,' said Fellows. 'Winchesters fetch premium.'

Azul stuffed bills into the man's vest. 'Show us,' he said. 'Fast.'

They went out the back of the bank, Tom wincing as his bare feet took splinters from the ground, and entered the store from the rear. Nathan Fellows brought ten rifles down from his racks and fetched boxes of shells from under the counter. Azul sent Billy Eagle to bring the horses up.

They loaded the rifles onto the two horses and turned to the three whitemen.

'That wasn't hard,' said Azul. 'Was it?'

Lomax, Tom and Nathan Fellows shook their heads.

'You all made a profit,' said Azul. 'Didn't you?'

The heads nodded in unison.

Azul said, 'So don't spread word. Or I'll come back. And kill you.'

The heads shook again.

'Fine.' Azul grinned as he climbed astride the grey stallion. 'That's what I call Indian trading.'

CHAPTER ELEVEN

'There's two men trailin' us.'

Billy Eagle sounded nervous.

'I know.' Azul went on riding at an easy pace. 'They been with us a week. Since just after Jameston.'

'You knew all along?' Now Billy sounded outraged. 'Christ! Why didn't you tell me? We could lose them.'

'No.' Azul shook his head. 'I don't want to.'

'What you talking about?' grunted Billy. 'You'll lead them straight to the gold.'

Azul nodded.

Billy frowned, reining in and twisting in his saddle to face Azul. He was sweating in the afternoon sun. He licked his lips and reached behind him to fetch a bottle from his saddlebags. Took a long swallow. A second.

'All right,' he said slowly, 'you want to tell me what's goin' on?'

Azul grinned. 'Joel Meek and Art Durant were waiting for us in Jameston. That'll be them behind us. Someone must've told them about our visit. I'd guess it was Lomax.'

'Shit!' Billy spat, his face suddenly pale. He drank more whiskey. 'An' you used my money to pay the bastard off! To keep his mouth shut.'

'You got plenty more,' Azul shrugged. 'Anyway, they won't be telling tales. And I don't reckon

Lomax will tell anyone else – he'd be risking his job if word got out he took a bribe to sell two halfbreeds new Winchesters.'

'So meanwhile we got two hired killers ridin' herd.' Billy shook his head; disbelievingly. 'An' you want to show them my gold.'

'They won't try anything until they know where the gold is,' said Azul calmly. 'And when they find it, I'm going to kill them. Besides, you got Chikisin and his broncos guarding the place.'

Billy mumbled something that sounded like *Shit!* It was hard to tell because his mouth was wrapped around the bottle again. Azul chuckled and urged the grey horse forwards. Billy followed on, still drinking.

They maintained a steady pace throughout the next two weeks, moving down the Gila and then cutting south to hit the Mamacita before climbing into the Piñon Llanos foothills. The two riders stayed resolutely behind them, mostly holding back by day and then moving up at night when Azul took care to build the campfire up high. Billy found comfort in his bottles, and some small degree of courage, too. He began, even, to appreciate the irony of the situation.

Azul remained calm. He was far enough out from Jameston that even if Lomax did hear the two men had been killed – which seemed unlikely – there would be nothing he could do about it. To prove that either Azul or Billy had killed the men would be impossible when they were riding into country holding hostile Apaches. Even if the bodies were found.

It reminded him of one of his first hunts with old Sees-The-Fox.

The Chiricahua had taken a group of Indian

youths to a wide valley high up in the Mogollons. They were after deer, and Sees-The-Fox had placed the youngsters at the narrower end of the valley, waiting.

They won't come down here, Azul had said. *They will know it could be a trap.*

Sees-The-Fox had chuckled and tugged a hide from his mustang. It was the hide of a big buck, the antlers still attached. He had draped it over his shoulders, fastening the head-piece over his hair so that the antlers stuck out behind. When he got down on his knees, the empty legs fastened to his wrists and ankles, he looked like a deer.

Listen, he had said, *deer are like men in some ways. They are nervous, but they are also curious. And sometimes, they are greedy. If you understand that, then you can use it. You can make them forget the danger of a trap.*

Then he had crawled down the slope and out into the valley. From the height, he looked for all the world like a browsing deer. He made the right movements and the right sounds. And after a while, a small herd had come wandering up to find out what was so interesting that the big twelve-point stag was finding.

The youths had taken five does, sufficient to feed the whole *rancheria* for weeks.

You see? The old man had asked Azul. *Do you understand now?*

I think so, the boy had replied. *Sometimes it is better to lure than to ride down.*

That is part of it, Sees-The-Fox said. *But first you must understand the thing you hunt. A deer, a buffalo, a man — you must know their weakness and use it against them.*

The way Azul saw it now, his pursuers had two

weaknesses that were leading them straight into a trap. One was their lust for the gold – or whatever share Stanton had promised them – and the other was their hatred for him. The two, combined, were luring them to him as surely as Sees-The-Fox had brought the deer in on that long-ago day.

One day out from Billy's camp he speeded the pace. One of Chikisin's warriors met them.

'There are two *pinda-lick-oyi* behind you,' he said. 'But I suppose you know that.'

Azul nodded. 'I want them alive. They belong to me.'

The bronco grunted and produced a small metal mirror. He turned the polished face to the sun and flashed a message in the swift code of the Apache. It was answered from higher up the slope. Azul grinned, knowing the message would reach all of Chikisin's guards: long before the Americans began to use the heliograph, the Apaches had perfected the art of sending messages by the sun.

'We brought the rifles,' he said. 'I will give them to Chikisin.'

'He is waiting for you,' answered the brave. 'With Naize and Cicatriz.'

Azul and Billy Eagle continued on to the meadow. The three Indians were hunkered down at the far end. They smiled when they saw the guns packed on the horses.

'You brought them,' said Chikisin. *'Enjuh!'*

'What has happened?' asked Azul. 'It seems too quiet.'

'There was a little fight.' Chikisin laughed. 'A band of seven *pinda-lick-oyi* got too close. So we killed them. We put them back on their horses and took them down to where there was another band. Then we put fire under the ponies' tails and sent them to the others with our message. It was great sport! The *pinda-lick-oyi* ran like frightened rabbits! There are no more up here now. Except the two the mirrors spoke of. What shall we do with them?'

'Catch them and bring them to me,' said Azul. 'Unharmed.'

Chikisin nodded and turned away, sending a signal up the slope.

'In the morning,' he said. 'I will bring them to you then.'

Art Durant tugged his blanket tighter about his shoulders against the dawn chill and blew on the smouldering fire. He was careful to avoid making smoke as he added fuel and set the coffee pot to boiling. He heated a separate billy of water and shaved. He wished he had a clean shirt.

Across the clearing, Joel Meek opened his eyes and sat up with the LeMat angling into the trees.

'You're spooky.' Durant's voice was soft, almost caressing. 'I give you a hard time?'

Meek grunted without speaking. He reached down to fasten his fly, then pushed the blanket aside. The two bedrolls were close together. He wiped a hand over his eyes and held out a cup. Durant poured coffee.

'We must be close now,' he said. 'Maybe tomorrow.'

'What do we do when we find it?' asked Durant. 'After we kill the 'breeds?'

'Light out,' answered Meek. 'Take as much as we can carry an' stash the rest.'

'Cole won't like that,' suggested Durant. 'Not at all.'

'Bugger Cole,' grunted Meek. 'We find that Spanish gold, we're takin' it.'

Durant giggled. 'We could go to New Orleans, Joel. Or Washington. Maybe even Paris, France. I read about that one time.'

'Yeah.' Meek thrust the LeMat into the holster. 'We gotta find it first, though. Let's go.'

Durant doused the fire with the undrunk coffee. Then he saddled both horses. Meek watched him gather up the bedrolls and stow them behind the saddles.

And I'll go alone, thought Durant. *In Paris, France, I can get some real nice clothes. And with money, I can have anyone I want.*

He was still thinking about it as they rode up the trail that wound, cork-screwing, to the next rise. The trail was overhung with dense timber. Oaks and cedar and aspen fought for space so that they moved through a tunnel of dim light that was loud with birdsong and sweet with the odour of dew-drenched sap.

Partway up an empty whisky bottle glinted in the light filtering through the trees. Farther on there was a tiny scrap of cloth hanging from a bush. Durant reined in, turning round to speak to Meek.

'They ain't coverin' their trail at all. That's odd.'

'They're close to home,' rumbled the giant man. 'They probably ain't takin' care. 'Breeds get messy when they think they're safe.'

Durant nodded and heeled his pony up the slope. Five hundred feet on he could see light coining golden discs against the trees where the slope gave out onto a meadow. He slipped his Winchester from the saddle boot and levered a shell into the breech. Behind him, he heard the hammer of the LeMat snap back.

Then he heard the massive pistol blast its load of 18 bore shot against the trees. Leaves fluttered loose about his face as he turned. He heard a crow lift rasping into the sky. A bluejay shriek a protest.

Joel Meek was down on his back. His arms were pinned against his body by a lariat. There was a second around his neck and a third dragging his right foot off to the side.

As Durant turned, something landed about his shoulders. His horse bucked as Meek's ran past. The force tightened, pinning his arms and dragging him sideways. The Winchester exploded a useless shell against the sky and he was falling from the pony. The ground hit him like a locomotive slamming into the buffers, and the Winchester burst from his hands. The rope dragged tight as he tried to struggle to his feet. A second pinned his ankles together.

Then three men came out from the trees. They all had long, black hair and Winchester rifles. One had a broken nose and a scar running down his face. Durant watched them run over to Joel Meek and drive the stocks of the rifles against the big man's face and belly. Joel roared, then went quiet. Art tried to work his hands down to where he could grip the two S & W Schofields, but before he even had a chance a rifle stock landed against the side of his head and he got swept down inside a long spiral of whirling red that ended in darkness.

When he opened his eyes again he was in a canyon. There was grass under him and warmth against his back from a sun-heated rockface. There was a tall man staring at him. A man with a mane of sun-bleached blond hair that was fastened back from his face by a leather band. The man was dressed in a faded linen shirt and a dark leather vest. He wore tight-fitting buckskin pants that were tucked inside knee-high Apache-style moccasins. There was a gunbelt around the man's waist. It held a Colt's Frontier model tied down on the right side, and a big Bowie knife on the left. The man's eyes were very blue. They were also very cold. Art Durant shuddered when he saw the look in the eyes. It was like looking into his own grave.

He tried to stand up. And realised that he was tied, wrists to ankles, with a pole thrust under his knees.

'I am Azul,' said the man. 'Once you beat me. Now I am going to kill you.'

Sweat beaded Durant's forehead and he looked round for Joel Meek.

The giant was tied in the same way. There were three Apaches pointing new-looking Winchesters at his face as it purpled with his efforts to break free.

'Oh, Christ!' Art said softly. Then louder: 'Oh, Christ! Please! Don't.'

'Maybe not,' said the tall man. 'I will give you a chance.'

His voice was very cold. It frightened Durant as much as the eyes. There was hate in it, along with implacable purpose. Like a grave-digger's shovel dropping soil on a dead man's face.

'Cut him free.'

Durant felt his bonds part under the slicing of a keen-bladed knife. He stood up, massaging his wrists.

'I will give you back both your guns,' said Azul. 'When you are ready.'

Durant looked round. To his left he saw Billy Eagle, grinning as he held the twin-holstered belt. To his right there was another Apache with a Winchester angled at his stomach. Behind Azul, there were two more Indians, both holding rifles cocked in his direction.

'If I win?' he asked, not believing it. 'What then?'

'You go free.' Azul's voice was harsh with the guttural accents of Apacheria, with an overlay of his father's Scottish burr. 'No one will stop you.'

Durant massaged his wrists.

He rubbed them carefully. He kneaded his fingers. Azul waited.

Durant saw no other way out. He nodded.

'All right. I'm ready.'

Billy Eagle passed him his gunbelt. Durant buckled it on. He fastened the thongs around his thighs. Let his fingers drift over the butts.

'How do I know they're loaded?' he asked.

'Check them,' said Azul.

Durant thought about chancing a sneak shot. Then he looked at the rifles pointed in his direction and changed his mind. He lifted both guns, sliding the catch clear of the rear frame so that shells snapped loose on the automatic ejector system. He picked each one up. Cleaned it as he checked it, and slid it back into the chambers before dropping the pistols back inside the holsters.

'Call it,' said Azul.

Art Durant lifted both Schofields at the same time. His thumbs closed on the hammers and his forefingers snapped down on the triggers. He was fast. Very fast.

Azul saw the pistols lift as his own hand fisted the butt of the Colt's Frontier. His thumb closed down on the hammer, cocking the pistol as it lifted from the holster. At the same time, his forefinger hooked through the trigger guard, taking the trigger back so that all that held the revolver off of firing was the slight pressure of his thumb against the hammer. As the muzzle lined on Art Durant's stomach, he let the hammer slip.

The Colt bucked in his hand.

There was the familiar blast of the .45 calibre shell.

A wash of flame riding out in front of a cloud of smoke.

He held the trigger down as he thumbed the hammer a second time.

Once is dead. Twice is safe.

Art Durant went back with his mouth wide open and his eyes staring at the sky. What was left of them.

Azul's first bullet took the fancy-dressed man one inch above his belt. It entered through the muscle and tore into the intestines, ripping them open before striking one of the lower, hindward ribs to shatter the bone and drive it outwards. Art Durant screamed. He doubled over with long trailers of bloody vomit spilling from his mouth as the enormous hole in his back gouted a spray of crimsoned bone and sticky pieces of entrail. The second bullet hit his face as he jacknifed over. It struck between his eyes, glancing off the bone to enter his face on the left side of his cheek. It tore down into the flesh, sharding his upper teeth into fragments of blood-spattered bone and enamel that fountained from his mouth like fireworks on the Fourth of July. It pierced his lower jaw and scored a bloody line down his chest.

Durant jerked back under the impact. His face was a mask of blood. His eyes were squinted inwards where the bullet had fragmented bone, and where it had entered his cheek there was a great scarlet wash coming from the hole. His lips were open, pulped and shredded under the force of the bullet and his own nervous twitching. His teeth were sharded stumps. Thick pulses of blood pumped from under his jaw. He slammed back against the rockface and slumped sideways. Where he had been, there were long crimson marks. The grass under his corpse got red. Flies began to buzz.

Azul opened the loading gate of the Colt and thumbed the spent cartridges free. He reloaded. Turned to Joel Meek.

'Art don't make a pretty picture,' he said. 'Colourful though.'

'You goddam halfbreed bastard!' Meek struggled against the ropes, ignoring the pointed rifles. 'You fuckin' squaw turd! Wait until the judge gets this. He'll sign that mine over to Stanton an' get the Army to clear you red nigger bastard spawn outta here. It won't be long.'

Foam frothed over his lips, and his eyes bulged from his head. Azul laughed.

'What judge?' he said. 'I'm the only judge around here.'

'Abel Cantwell,' snarled Meek. 'He's due any time now. He gets word of this, you don't have a chance.'

'Thanks,' said Azul, 'thanks a lot. That's just what I wanted to know.' He nodded to Chikisin. 'Send your warriors out. Like I told you.'

'Now?' asked the Apache, looking disappointed.

'After,' said Azul. 'Cut him loose first.'

Chikisin reached down to slash through Joel Meek's bonds.

The giant came up on his feet in a surge of movement. He lifted Chikisin and threw him against Cicatriz. The two Apaches tumbled to the ground, stunned. Meek ducked his head and rammed into

Azul. The halfbreed felt the wind gust clear of his lungs as his back hit the grass. He looked up in time to see Meek snatch Chikisin's rifle and blast fast shots into the startled warriors moving in on the fight. One went down with a bullet through his stomach, groaning as he cupped his hands over the hole. Another clutched at a bleeding shoulder, and the third spun round and dropped as the .44-40 slug grazed the side of his head.

Joel Meek took off at a run faster than any man that big had a right to move.

He went through the ponies penned inside the canyon, his yelling, screaming passage spooking the animals so that they began to mill around, covering his escape. He got to the entrance of the canyon and ducked under the fence lines, running down the trail into the trees.

Azul picked up a fallen Winchester and began to run after the giant.

Behind him, he heard Chikisin shout, 'We'll ride him down.'

He paused long enough to shout back: 'No! He's mine!'

And then he was out of the meadow and pacing fast after Joel Meek.

His chest ached where the giant man had hit him. He ignored it. Ignored all the pain as he ran down through the trees, his mind working fast. Working out where Meek would stop: the best place for an ambush.

He halted, panting, and climbed up the loamy slope, using the out-thrust roots of the oaks and cedar and aspen to reach the higher ground. Then he paced forwards. Like some great cat, cautious; determined.

He paced along the ridge, listening for sounds from below. After a while, he heard the sound of heavy breathing and saw Joel Meek running through the trees.

The giant man was sweating heavily. His black beard was straggled over his chin, and his hair was plastered back against his skull. A bald spot showed at the apex.

Azul grinned and ran on, cutting in front of Meek where the trail curved round a long outcrop of rock that was banded on two sides by high stands of impenetrable timber. On the other by a fall of shale. He went down through the trees and dropped onto the trail where it wound round the farthest line of the drop.

After a while, Meek showed. He was panting; inside his eyes there were lines of tears that ran down to join the sweat on his face.

'You can't get away,' said Azul.

Joel Meek lifted his Winchester and triggered a single shot.

Azul went sideways against the dirt wall. He fired his own rifle as he fell.

The bullet hit Joel Meek in the left shoulder. It punctured the bone and ripped up the trapezoid muscle. The giant's left arm snatched rigid, jumping out to the side with his numbed fingers flying clear of the rifle.

He used his right arm to lever the gun again, snatching the grip down and snapping it back as his finger closed on the trigger. The Winchester barked as Azul rolled over the trail, fetching up against the edge of the steep, shale covered slope. He fired as he rolled. His bullet hit Joel Meek in the left knee. It shattered the cap, spraying shards of bone and blood out through the big man's pants. Meek screamed and fell down on his right side.

He still held the rifle. There was froth on his face, soaking down into his beard. The ground underneath him was thick with blood. He lifted his good arm, trying to cock the Winchester again.

Azul shot him in the wrist.

The delicate bones shattered against the dirt. Joel Meek screamed as his right hand lurched clear of his arm. Long, thin streamers of blood ran from the veins. Then the arteries pulsed open, gouting enormous floods from the severed arm.

Joel Meek looked up at Azul and said, 'You bastard.'

Azul looked down at the dying eyes and said, 'I made a promise.'

Then he kicked Joel Meek in the belly, sending the body over the rim of the shale wash.

There was a sudden, upright, gust of blood as the man went over. It splattered on Azul's moccasins. The halfbreed ignored it as he watched the body tumble down the slope.

Meek screamed as he fell into the shale and began to slide downwards. The loose rock went with him. Like a blanket.

Like a shroud.

It covered the stump of his arm and the hole in his shoulder. It covered his eyes and his mouth. It covered his screaming, blocking off his cries behind a curtain of falling, blood-drenched chips.

As he fell, his body dislodged fresh falls, so that when he reached the bottom he was covered under a shifting grey mass of stone and dust.

Azul watched until the dust was cleared. There was nothing below except the steadily settling bank

of shale. There was no sign of Joel Meek. Nothing.
The halfbreed looked down.

'I guess,' he murmured, 'the Meek inherited the earth.'

CHAPTER TWELVE

Cole Stanton raised his glass, holding it to the light. He nodded thoughtfully and sipped the wine. He dabbed his lips with a napkin, then filled the glass of the man across the table. The room was dim, save for the glow of the kerosene lantern suspended from the ceiling. The wick of that was turned down low and the radiance was diffused through an ornate shade of paper-thin abalone. The table was draped with a spotless white cloth. Silver cutlery glistened with a bright, metallic sheen that contrasted with the rich ruby colour of the wine.

The man facing Stanton tasted the vintage and nodded approvingly. He was a short man, around fifty, with snow-white hair and a pot belly thrusting out his dark vest. A gold watch-chain spanned his stomach. He wore a crisp white shirt with a starched collar and a tidily knotted string tie. He smiled at Stanton.

'You've done well for yourself out here.'

Stanton shrugged. 'It's not too bad. The climate is healthy.'

'Here's to health.' The white-haired man raised his glass.

'And wealth,' Stanton added.

'Of which there's a great deal,' murmured the man. 'If the rumours I've been hearing are true.'

'Exactly what have you heard, Judge?' Stanton sliced meat. 'Rumours are cheap in these parts.'

'Rumours are cheap anywhere.' Judge Abel Cantwell forked peas into his mouth. It was a small, prim-looking mouth. 'I prefer facts.'

Stanton chewed slowly. Swallowed. Sipped wine. Waited.

At last Cantwell said, 'Spanish gold. The way I heard the story, some halfbreed located a cache. Two hunters got close and he killed them. Vance Cobly arrested the halfbreed when he came in wearing the guns of one of the dead men. He had a friend – another halfbreed – and they broke jail together. That's as much as I know.'

'The halfbreed is called Billy Eagle,' murmured Stanton. 'The two men he killed worked for me. They were out after game, but I guess they got too close to Billy's camp. The other one is called Azul. I believe he is also known as Breed. He pistol-whipped the sheriff when they got away.'

Cantwell nodded thoughtfully. 'There was talk of a massacre.'

'Yes.' Stanton poured more wine from the crystal decanter. 'I volunteered the services of some of my men. They were all killed.'

'Witnesses?' asked the judge. 'Anyone see it?'

'No.' Stanton shook his head. 'They all died. There was a second attack a few weeks ago. That was witnessed.'

'The halfbreeds did it?' demanded Cantwell. 'They were seen?'

Stanton dabbed at his mouth. 'Not in person. The attackers were Apaches.'

Cantwell grunted. 'This is Apache country, Mr. Stanton. Those hills are full of broncos.'

'Billy Eagle and Breed are both half-Apache.' Stanton poured gravy over mashed potato. 'They must have help.'

'That's an opinion.' Cantwell shook his white-haired head. 'I deal in facts.'

'Fact is that Billy admitted killing my men,' said Stanton evenly. 'He was boasting about it. Fact is that both halfbreeds broke jail, assaulting Sheriff Cobly in the process.'

'It seems odd,' murmured Cantwell, 'that the man should come here boasting about it. Carrying a dead man's guns.'

'Billy's a drunk.' Stanton emptied the decanter. 'He spends his money on cheap liquor and cheap women.'

'In your saloon, I understand.' Cantwell's voice was dry. 'The Little Sister.'

Stanton shrugged. 'It's a business enterprise. My interest is purely financial.'

'Of course.' Cantwell's blue eyes twinkled. Perhaps with amusement. 'But Billy Eagle has disappeared. There's nothing I can do about that except send a report to the Federal authorities, though I doubt they'll do anything.'

'Two of my best men are looking for him now,' said Stanton.

'Looking?' asked Cantwell. 'Or hunting?'

'Does it matter?' Stanton felt vaguely uneasy. 'They've been deputised.'

'Yes, so Cobly told me.' Cantwell smiled. It was impossible to tell if it was a friendly smile. 'Will they bring him in alive?'

Stanton shrugged without saying anything.

'The point is,' continued the judge, 'that without a trial I can't find Billy Eagle guilty. There are discrepancies in this case. I don't understand why a man – and especially a halfbreed – would let it be known he had killed two men. I need to question this Billy Eagle. And the one called Breed.'

Stanton began to cough. He turned away from the table as he fumbled a silk kerchief from the pocket of his black suit. Dark crimson spots appeared on the silk. After a while he stopped. His face had gone very pale. He folded the kerchief and put it back in his pocket, then he reached out to tug on a corded bell-pull. A Chinaman came through the door and began to clear the plates. A little while later he came back with two dishes of canned peaches and a jug of cream.

Cantwell spooned the sticky fruit into his mouth. Then he asked, 'Exactly what is your interest in all this, Mr. Stanton?'

'Justice,' said the cadaverous man. 'I want to see a killer brought to justice.'

'And the gold?' Again it was impossible to tell which way Cantwell's mind was working. 'Does that have nothing to do with it?'

Stanton shrugged. He wiped his mouth and pushed his plate away. Stood up, going over to the armoire to fetch a second decanter and two small, heavy glasses.

'Port,' he said. 'An excellent vintage. I'd offer you a cigar, but the smoke bothers me.'

Cantwell smiled, waving a plump-fingered hand. 'It doesn't matter. My question does.'

'About the gold?' Stanton filled the glasses with the ruby liquid. 'I'd be a dishonest man if I said I wasn't interested.'

'How much interested?' asked the judge.

'I'm a businessman,' said Stanton slowly, choosing his words with care. 'If I could find that gold, I could build an empire.'

'But Billy Eagle found it,' smiled Cantwell. 'Therefore it belongs to him.'

'But Billy Eagle,' said Stanton, 'is a self-confessed murderer. He'll hang.'

'Not without a trial, I hope.' Cantwell emptied his glass and pushed his chair back. 'I'd like to question the man before I reach any decision.'

He picked up his hat. It was a curly-brimmed beaver, a fraction too large for his small head.

'I must go now. I have some paperwork. I think I'll stay over a few days, in case your men bring Billy Eagle in.'

After the door had closed behind him, Stanton stood looking at it for a long time. His narrow lips writhed like fighting worms and he began to curse. He was very fluent, and it took him some time before he ran out of words. When he had, he picked up the decanter and topped his glass. He took the port in one fast swallow and began to cough again. His body spasmed, angular shoulders hiking up about his neck. His face went the colour of a dead fish's underbelly. Thin red veins stood out on his cheeks and in his eyes.

When he was finished, he wiped his mouth and stood staring down at the carpet. There were bright scarlet drops on the pattern.

Vance Cobly lifted the bottle and eased the neck cautiously between his lips. He took a long drink and set the whisky down on the floor beside him. His chair creaked slightly and he adjusted his weight as he felt a spring dig against his rump. Moonlight filtered in through the shuttered windows. It was the only light in the room. Cobly sighed and touched the bandages still covering his face.

He wasn't a bad lawman, he thought. At least, he

hadn't been until Cole Stanton put temptation his way. Hell! he was fifty years old – ancient for a peace officer – and what did he have to show for the last thirty years? A house that needed painting and the roof fixing before the winter rains. Exactly three hundred and fifty dollars and twenty cents in the bank that was owned by Stanton. A fine black quarter horse. A fine wife – yes, that was important : a very fine wife. No kids because a youngster with a fast temper and no head for liquor had put a .36 calibre slug through his belly and done something to his insides.

He reached inside his shirt, absently touching the puckered scar. There was another three inches higher on the right side. Two on his back. Two more on his left leg. And one on his right.

Thirty years a lawman, he thought, reaching for the bottle. Thirty years in grubby little cow towns and mining settlements. He'd forgotten the names of most of them. Didn't even want to remember. Except the scars forced names into his mind : Sedalia. Wichita. Kansas City. Tombstone. El Paso. Bandera. Taos. He'd worked with Hickock. With Masterson. With Stoudenmire. He'd gone up against rustlers and outlaws; against bank robbers and half-crazed gun-fighters.

And he'd wound up in Chandler's Butte depending on Cole Stanton for a job.

He'd never taken a bribe before. Never put a man in a cell, or under the ground, he didn't think deserved it.

Until now.

Until Cole Stanton came talking about Spanish gold and St. Louis houses. Dresses for Elizabeth. Peace for him.

The door opened and his wife came into the room.

Her hair was lost under a sleeping cap, and she had a faded robe clutched tight about her body.

'Vance?' she said, her voice soft; questioning. 'What's the trouble?'

'Couldn't sleep,' he muttered.

'So you sit up with a whisky bottle? That's not like you.'

'Hell! I got things on my mind, Lizzy.'

'Like what?'

'Nothing. It ain't yore problem.'

'You're my husband,' she said, coming to stand beside him, one hand stroking his grey hair. 'They're my problems, too.'

'Go back to bed, woman. I'll be up in a while.'

'It's Cole Stanton, isn't it?' She moved round to face him, pulling up a chair that needed its seat recovered. 'It's Billy Eagle and that other one. It's the gold.'

Her voice was quiet. Filled with concern. She reached out to touch his face, and he kissed her hand. There was a gentleness to her. A strength, too; the kind only a woman had : a kind of calm, sure centre that stood rock-steady through all the trials. Down all the years.

He shook his head and put the bottle down. And then it all came flooding out of him.

It felt good to tell it. Like lancing a pus-filled sore and feeling the poison drain away. Like waking after a bad dream and feeling the warm, safe body beside him.

When he was finished, his wife said, 'You've got to tell that Judge, Vance. Tell him everything. You've got to arrest Cole Stanton.'

Cobly rubbed at what parts of his face he could touch.

'Cole wasn't there,' he said wearily. 'He's too smart for that. It was always his men handled the killing. The judge won't be able to touch him. Besides, I'll lose my job.'

She took hold of his hands, staring into his eyes.

'Vance,' she said slowly, very clearly, 'you got more to lose than the job. I wed a man with respect. I want him to keep that.'

He looked at her. And for a moment, as a shard of moon's light fell across her face, all the years dropped away. He felt like weeping. Instead, he nodded.

'You're right, Lizzy. I'll do it in the morning.'

'Good,' she said. And led him by the hand into the bedroom.

'This is crazy,' grunted Billy Eagle. 'You're mad.'

Azul shook his head. 'It's the best way. Trust me.'

Billy shrugged. 'I guess you been right so far.'

Azul turned to Chikisin : 'You know what to do?' The Chiricahua nodded.

'*Enjuh!*' said Azul. 'Good.'

He slipped away into the darkness. Silent as a cat, moving from shadow into shadow, disappearing into the outskirts of Chandler's Butte like a wraith. Like a warrior of the Chiracahua on the hunt.

He darted through the streets, empty at this late hour, moving towards The Hotel.

There was a light burning outside, shedding faint radiance over the porch, swaying slightly in the night wind. He moved to the rear. Found the stairs down which Joel Meek and the others had taken him. He went up them.

The door was open : he went inside, into the corridor. He paced down the boards on silent, moccasined feet until he found the door to Stanton's rooms. Then he drew his Bowie knife and slid the blade into the lock, between the striker and the catch-plate. The door opened with a faint *click!* and he stepped inside.

The room was dark and quiet. There was a memory of food in the air. From behind the door to his left there came the sound of snoring. He went over to the door and eased it gently open.

The shutters were pegged back, the curtains rustling softly in the breeze. Two huge wardrobes covered most of one wall. Between them there was a wide, brass-railed bed. There was a dressing-table facing the bed. It had a swivel mirror and a built-in basin. Ivory-handled brushes and a straight razor were set out neatly on a strip of white linen with fancy embroidery along the edges. Medicine bottles glinted darkly. At the centre of the bed there was a humped shape. A red night cap was on the pillow.

Azul crossed the room and placed the blade of the Bowie against Stanton's throat.

The man groaned in his sleep and began to turn over. Azul put a hand, his left, over the man's mouth and pricked his neck. Stanton grunted. Azul pricked him again.

Stanton's eyes opened and he tried to sit up. Azul pushed him down, lifting the Bowie so that the moonlight reflected off the blade. He set the cutting edge against Stanton's cheek.

'Don't call out.' His voice was soft and ugly. 'Don't try anything.'

'You're dead.' Stanton's voice was harsh, almost as lifeless as his face. 'You'll never get away with it.'

'The Judge,' said Azul. 'Where's the Judge?'

'Cantwell?' Stanton squinted at the blade pressing against his eye socket. 'Two doors down.'

'Get up.' Azul eased the knife back. 'Take me to him.'

He kept the Bowie close to Stanton's face as the thin man climbed from the bed, then grabbed a handful of nightshirt and rested the blade on Stanton's shoulder, pressing against the neck. Stanton moved awkwardly to the door.

'He'll hang you,' said the consumptive. 'That's why he's here.'

'We'll see,' murmured Azul. 'Though you'll not be there.'

He shoved Stanton up against the door and slid the Bowie back in the sheath. He drew his Colt and rapped the barrel against the wood. A sleep-filled voice asked, 'Who's there?' Azul nudged Stanton with the pistol and the cadaverous man said, 'Me, judge. Cole Stanton.'

'What you want?'

Azul nudged Stanton again and the man said, 'I have to see you. It's urgent.'

Cantwell muttered something and bedsprings creaked. Then the door opened.

Azul shoved Stanton through and swung in fast, heeling the door closed behind him.

Cantwell was dressed in a blue-and-white striped nightshirt. His white hair stood out crooked from his scalp. His eyes were fudged with sleep. Azul pushed him back, leaning against the door as he angled the Colt between the two men.

'I am Azul,' he said.

Cantwell's mouth opened, then closed fast. The sleep went out of his eyes. He said, 'Jesus!' Then: 'What the hell you want?'

'You came here to try Billy Eagle,' said Azul. 'Me, too. Do you know why?'

Cantwell sat down on the bed. His legs were too short for his feet to touch the floor. He shrugged. 'I know what you're accused of.'

'Billy Eagle didn't kill anyone,' said Azul. 'I did.'

'You giving yourself up?' Cantwell reached over to the washstand to collect a pair of gold-rimmed spectacles. He hooked them over his ears.

Azul shook his head. 'The first two were called Donny and Osmond,' he said. 'Stanton sent them to trail Billy. To find the gold. They ambushed him. I saw them and killed them.'

'The first two?' asked Cantwell. 'That mean there are more?'

Azul nodded. 'A man called Jimmy Witt. Stanton sent him and a gang of hired guns after us when we broke jail. I was supposed to lead them to Billy's gold after Stanton and Cobly let us escape.'

'And you killed them?' said Cantwell. 'All of them?'

'They didn't leave much choice,' said Azul.

'Hired guns?' asked the judge. 'All of them?'

'Like Joel Meek and Art Durant,' Azul nodded. 'I killed them, too.'

'No!' Stanton gaped. 'You can't! They were the best. I sent them . . .'

His voice tailed off as Cantwell's pudgy face swivelled in his direction. Suddenly the elderly judge didn't look like a little white-haired man in a nightshirt any more.

'Sent them?' he asked. 'To do what?'

Stanton began to cough. Down deep in his lungs something seemed to give way and he doubled over, clutching at his chest. Blood flecked his nightshirt and his whole body shook with the effort of breath. Cantwell passed him a towel and then a glass of water.

'I think,' he said, 'that I better hear both sides of this.'

Morning filtered light through the shutters. Azul was still on his feet. Still holding the gun. Cantwell was seated on the edge of the bed with a notepad in his hand and a furiously scribbling pencil. Stanton slumped with a blanket draped over his shoulders. Somewhere to the east a cock crowed, the strident sound answered by a yelping dog.

'This is dirty,' said Cantwell. 'I don't like it.'

'Nor did Billy,' grunted Azul.

Cantwell swung his feet to the floor, looking up at the halfbreed. 'I'll convene a trial right after I've had breakfast.'

'Where?' Azul asked.

'Here's as good a place as any,' said the judge. 'In the lobby.'

'No.' Azul shok his head. 'Outside in the street. That way everyone hears the verdict.'

Cantwell stared up into the cold, calm blue eyes and nodded. 'All right. As you say. Now let me get dressed. Mr. Stanton, too.'

Azul nodded and holstered the Colt. He went over to the window and threw the shutters open. Then he drew the Bowie knife and held it out the window. Sunlight slanted off the blade as he shifted the axis, waving his left hand over the gleaming steel. From the far side of Chandler's Butte there came answering flashes.

'What the devil was that?' demanded Cantwell.

'Protection,' said Azul. 'Just in case.'

He turned to Stanton. 'Don't try to escape. It wouldn't be worth it.'

Stanton looked back at him with dead eyes. They held as much life as a boiled fish's. 'You goddam half-breed bastard,' he said. Quietly; tonelessly.

Azul smiled without showing any humour. 'See you at the trial.'

There was a desk set up at the centre of mainstreet. It was a wide, multi-drawered construction of polished teak, carried out from The Hotel along with the matching chair. Judge Abel Cantwell occupied the chair. He had his notepad in front of him and a neat brass inkwell with three metal-nibbed pens set out alongside. In front of the desk there were four chairs. Azul, Billy Eagle, Cole Stanton, and Vance Cobly sat on the chairs. The jury was lined up on the sidewalk. The rest of the citizens of Chandler's Butte stood or sat wherever they could get a view.

Beyond them, at vantage points on the roofs and in the alleys, there were Chikisin's Apaches. Each warrior held a brand-new Winchester.

Cantwell called for Billy Eagle to give evidence.

Then Azul.

Then Cole Stanton.

Then Sheriff Vance Cobly.

Cobly turned to face the crowd before he spoke. He saw his wife's face looking at him and smiled. Then he swung round to face Cantwell. His shoulders went back and he stood very straight. Through the muffling of the bandages his voice was clear.

'Cole owns this town. Most of it, at least. He wanted to own more. When he found that Billy Eagle had located that Spanish gold, he wanted that, too. He sent Osmond and Donny out to track the half-breed back to his camp. To kill him, if need be. When they got killed, he brought Joel Meek in to stir up trouble. To frighten Billy into telling. Billy didn't frighten, so Cole made a proposition to Azul: he

144

wanted him to talk with Billy an' find where the gold was hid. Azul refused, so Cole had his boys – Jimmy Witt, Art Durant, an' Joel Meek – work him over. They done a godawful job: he was a mess. Then Cole said we should let them break out. Azul fooled him into thinking he was going along with that, but he didn't. They broke out. An' I knew all about it. But they just headed for the hills an' got lost. Cole sent men after them, but they couldn't find the cache. So he sent Meek an' Durant to Jameston because he reckoned Billy would bank his gold there. I don't know what happened to them, but I guess they got killed trying to find Billy's camp.

'That's about it. Except I wish I never gone along with Cole. I never thought to go crawlin' under a snake's belly.'

Cantwell banged his gavel on the desk as the crowd began to talk.

When it got silent, he said: 'We have three indictments here. I will read them to you, and await your verdict.

'One: the murder charge against Billy Eagle. How find you?'

'Not guilty,' said the foreman of the jury.

'Two: the charge of homicide and jail-breaking against the halfbreed known as Azul. How find you?'

'Not guilty,' said the foreman.

'Three: the charge of wilful coercion in murder, theft, and jail-breaking against Cole Stanton. How find you?'

There was a long pause. The jury talked together. Some pointed at Stanton, some at the Apaches.

Then the foreman got up on his feet and said, 'Guilty.'

Stanton's face seemed to fall in on itself. His cheeks

got hollow and his eyes went blank. He lifted a kerchief from his pocket and dabbed at his mouth.

Cantwell said, 'Cole Stanton, I find you guilty as charged. I hereby sentence you to life imprisonment in the State Penitentiary. Sheriff, take him away.'

Vance Cobly looked surprised.

'You want me to do that? After what I told you?'

'You're still the peace officer,' said Cantwell. 'I'll consider the charges against you later.'

Cobly stood up: 'All right, judge. Thanks.'

He turned to Stanton: 'Come on, Cole.'

'The hell!' Stanton lifted to his feet with a little Remington over-and-under in his hand.

The muzzle spat flame and Vance Cobly went back with a .41 calibre ball plucking his life out of his belly. The slug hit him directly over the scar on his stomach. It puckered the lips of the old wound inwards and tore up his intestines as it ploughed through the fat and the muscle to puncture the softer stuff inside. A spurt of crimson gouted from the front of his body, then he jerked back as the slug smashed against a rib and deflected upwards into a kidney. Cobly's hand dropped away from the butt of his Remington as he went down on his knees. He pressed both hands tight against his belly. Blood came out from between his fingers. More came from his mouth. Under his shirt, a spill of intestines writhed like snakes, bulging out the material as it got dark with the outpouring of his life. He shook his head. Said, 'Lizzy,' and then his eyes closed.

He went forwards slowly, head drooping down like a tired mule. It touched the ground, the dirt around pooling with the blood coming from his mouth. Then his legs straightened, scuffing dirt, and he measured his length over the grubby street.

Stanton turned, angling the little Derringer on Azul.

The halfbreed had his Colt in his hand. The hammer was back and the trigger closed down.

Then his hand froze as a woman's voice shouted, 'No!'

And a gun roared, detonated a slug into the back of Cole Stanton's skull. It was a .41 calibre slug. Fired from an ancient Colt's Dragoon. It hit the back of Stanton's skull like a cannon ball. The entire bone structure sharded inwards, fragments of bone bursting through the softer matter of the brain. It came out between the eyes on a thick spray of crimson-coated fragments of bone and pulpy matter that was both brain and eyes. Stanton's face opened up. His pale skin was abruptly drenched in blood and streamers of sticky brain. The Derringer dropped, unfired, from his hand. He tottered forwards, the hole in his face pointed at the sky. Someone screamed.

Then he fell down. His knees buckled and his arms slumped to either side of his thin body. Like a tree withered by drought, he fell into the street. Blood splashed from the impact and from the hole in the back of his head there spurted a gout of crimson-covered brain matter. A fly landed on the reddened hair. It was swiftly joined by others.

Azul looked across the street to where Elizabeth Cobly stood weeping, the big old Dragoon clutched in both her hands.

Judge Abel Cantwell banged his gavel hard on the teak desk.

'Case closed,' he yelled. 'That's it.'

Azul holstered the Colt. He looked down at Cole Stanton's corpse and the body of Vance Cobly. Then over to Billy Eagle.

'I guess it's finished,' he said. 'I guess that's it.'

He swung round to wave at Chikisin, signalling the Apache warrior to leave. Then he went to where his horse was tethered and climbed astride the big grey stallion and rode away.

Three days later, judge Abel Cantwell left Chandler's Butte. He sent in a report to the Federal authorities that exonerated Vance Cobly, so his widow got a pension. It wasn't enough to live on, but at Cantwell's suggestion Billy Eagle gave her one gold bar. She used it to bury her husband and, after selling their place in Chandler's Butte, bought a small house on the outskirts of St. Louis. She had a cousin there. She lived in St. Louis for the rest of her life. When she died, her cousin was surprised to learn that she had three hundred and fifty dollars and twenty cents in the bank and a codicil to her will. It said that everything she owned went to the cousin, whose name was Mabel, if she arranged for Elizabeth to be buried in Chandler's Butte, alongside her husband. Mabel's children arranged it.

Part of Cantwell's report cleared Azul, Billy Eagle, and any companions of theirs, of all charges. They were all free men, with nothing against them.

Billy Eagle gave Chikisin four gold bars that the bronco traded at exorbitant rates for guns. Six months later, Cicatriz was killed in an attack on a Mexican horse ranch. Naize got shot by Texas Rangers when the band fled from the *Federales* and tried to steal fresh mounts from a stage station near El Paso. The station was owned by the S.A.W. line. Chikisin went onto the Warm Springs reservation and began to drink whisky. He married three Chiricahua women and then took a Yaqui wife. When he was drunk one night, a jealous wife slit his throat. Three days later the Indian police arrested a Chiricahua woman who said she was trying to reach Geronimo's broncos, because Goklya knew how to act like a real Apache. They let her go.

Billy Eagle collected his money together and went to live in New Orleans. He arrived with three trunks full of money. He bought a house and a team of fancy horses. He was enough of a talking point that he got invited to society parties. As a joke. He filled his house with seven whores, and when he got bored with them – or they with him – he changed them for a fresh consignment. He began to drink wine and imported whisky. Without the *e*. He boasted of finding the Spanish gold and shifting the hoard to a new location known only to him and a man called Breed. He never told anyone where that location was. Not even the girl he finally married : a large-breasted blonde from the red-plush stable of Madame Alicia de la Toure. Her name was Yvette, and when Billy died of alcohol poisoning one damp February morning he laughed as she asked him where the rest of the gold was hidden. Then he squeezed her right breast and choked out his life.

Azul was the only one who knew about the Spanish gold.

And he didn't want to know about it.

He had seen it and had some idea of just how much it was worth : more than he could comprehend. More than most people living around the Border could understand.

He left it where Billy had hidden it, and rode away in the direction of the Mogollons : it was too much trouble.

And no one ever found the fabled gold again.
Maybe it's still there.

WARLORDS

BY BOB LANGLEY

BRITAIN'S FUTURE?

Britain is on the verge of total collapse. North Sea oil has
suddenly run dry. Rationing and unemployment spread like
wildfire. And four elections in two months have plunged the
nation into a terrifying chaos.

Across the Atlantic America decides it is time to step in and
assist their one-time ally. BY FERMENTING NO LESS
THAN A FULL-SCALE BLOODY REVOLUTION
GUARANTEED TO BRING THE DYING NATION
TO HER KNEES AND TO CHANGE THE COURSE OF
WORLD HISTORY WITH ONE DEVASTATING,
FINAL COUP DE GRÂCE . . .

Fast and furious, WARLORDS is a terrifying and disturbing
vision of Britain at the mercy of the powerlords in the
not-so-distant future!

ADVENTURE THRILLER   0 7221 5409 7   £1.25

Book Tokens

**Give them
the pleasure of choosing**

Book Tokens can be bought
and exchanged at most
bookshops.

BY REASON OF INSANITY

BY SHANE STEVENS

KILLER ON THE PROWL ...

Victim from birth of grotesque physical and mental torture, Thomas Bishop believes he is the son of the notorious Caryl Chessman, executed kidnapper and rapist.

Bishop has already murdered his mother — and suffered the sentence society imposed on him. Now, aged twenty-five, he free to take his revenge on the female sex responsible for sending his father to the gas chamber. Wielding a surgeon's scalpel, Bishop murders women and mutilates their bodies in order to possess them in the only way he can. Leaving a trail of carnage in his wake, Thomas Bishop is intent on becoming the greatest mass-murderer America has ever seen. As the body-count mounts higher and a massive manhunt fails to locate its prey, it looks like Bishop will succeed ...

BY REASON OF INSANITY —
THE MOST SHATTERING EPIC EVER OF
MASS MURDER AND DESPERATE PURSUIT

CRIME   0 7221 8163 9   £1.75

A selection of bestsellers from **SPHERE**

FICTION

STEPPING	Nancy Thayer	£1.25	☐
THE GRAIL WAR	Richard Monaco	£1.75	☐
UNHOLY CHILD	Catherine Breslin	£1.75	☐
TO LOVE AGAIN	Danielle Steel	£1.25	☐
THE ELDORADO NETWORK	Derek Robinson	£1.50	☐

FILM AND TV TIE-INS

LLOYD GEORGE	David Benedictus	£1.25	☐
THE EMPIRE STRIKES BACK	Donald F. Glut	£1.00	☐
CLOSE ENCOUNTERS OF THE THIRD KIND	Steven Spielberg	85p	☐
BUCK ROGERS IN THE 25TH CENTURY	Addison E. Steele	95p	☐
BUCK ROGERS 2: THAT MAN ON BETA	Addison E. Steele	95p	☐

NON-FICTION

A MATTER OF LIFE	R. Edwards & P. Steptoe	£1.50	☐
SUPERLEARNING	Sheila Ostrander & Lynn Schroeder with Nancy Ostrander	£1.75	☐
SPACE	Martin Ince	£1.50	☐
MENACE: The Life and Death of the Tirpitz	Ludovic Kennedy	£1.25	☐

All Sphere books are available at your local bookshop or newsagent, or can be ordered direct from the publisher. Just tick the titles you want and fill in the form below.

Name _____

Address _____

Write to Sphere Books, Cash Sales Department, P.O. Box 11, Falmouth, Cornwall TR10 9EN
Please enclose cheque or postal order to the value of the cover price plus:
UK: 25p for the first book plus 12p per copy for each additional book ordered to a maximum charge of £1.05.
OVERSEAS: 40p for the first book and 12p for each additional book.
BFPO & EIRE: 25p for the first book plus 10p per copy for the next 8 books, thereafter 5p per book.

Sphere Books reserve the right to show new retail prices on covers which may differ from those previously advertised in the text or elsewhere, and to increase postal rates in accordance with the PO.